KEEP IT HUMBLE!

The pitch came into the low inside strike zone. It was a tough pitch to hit, but Robbie Belmont was ready. He swung with pure joy, barely feeling a thing in his bat as he swatted the ball. There was just a sweet crunch.

The whole Riverton Tigers team stopped to watch the ball sail deeper and deeper. It was a powerful shot, a clean homer. Robbie trotted around the bases, tilting his head slightly down. He was thinking, *Humble! Keep it humble!* while nearly bursting with satisfaction.

GARY CARTER'S
IR⚾N MASK

HOME RUN!

by Robert Montgomery

Troll Associates

Library of Congress Cataloging-in-Publication Data

Montgomery, Robert, (date)
  Home run! / by Robert Montgomery; illustrated by Ralph Reese.
    p.   cm.—(Gary Carter's iron mask; 1)
  Summary: Yearning to show what he can do as a pitcher for his high
school baseball team, fifteen-year-old Robbie is dismayed when the
coach decides to make him catcher instead.
  ISBN 0-8167-1986-1 (lib. bdg.)   ISBN 0-8167-1987-X (pbk.)
  [1. Baseball—Fiction.] I. Reese, Ralph, ill.   II. Title.
III. Series: Montgomery, Robert, 1946-   Gary Carter's iron mask;
1.
PZ7.H76854Ho   1991
[Fic]—dc20   89-5190

Copyright © 1991 by Troll Associates, Mahwah, N.J.

10 9 8 7 6 5 4 3 2 1

INTRODUCTION

by Gary Carter

Baseball is America's game.

More people play and watch baseball than any other sport in the United States. It's the sport that most people outside the United States think of when they think of us. A wise man once said that if you want to understand America, first you must understand baseball. He also said that the best place to start is in small towns.

The major leagues show baseball at its *best*. But it's in the small-town parks that we can find baseball at its purest. That's where people play the game just for the joy it brings.

And it does bring joy. I've been blessed with the ability to play baseball well enough to make a living at it. But I would play baseball anyway for the pleasure of the game.

One thing I know for sure: Baseball takes individual and team effort both. And the accent is on *team*. Baseball isn't one against one like boxing. It's a group of individuals working closely together for a common goal. That's why the dream of baseball is still the traditional dream of America. Fairness, hard work, doing your best—those aren't just words. They can and still do lead to success, on and off the field.

It's no surprise, then, that Robbie Belmont's story—the story of the Iron Mask series and *Home Run!* here—is a little old-fashioned. I like that. *I'm* a little old-fashioned. Robbie has set himself a tough goal, and it's a goal he'll have to earn. No one is going to give him a job playing major-league baseball if he hasn't shown that he can do it. And if he shows that he can do it, it will be very tough to stop him.

Baseball places a lot of emphasis on *earning* what you get. If you get on base because a fielder made a mistake, you don't get credit for a hit. There are six ways of reaching first base when you're at bat: a hit, a walk, an error, being hit by a pitch, a balk, and catcher's interference. But only one of these ways raises your batting average: a hit. And what is the most important statistic for pitchers? Their *earned* run average!

There's no question that Robbie will have to work on his baseball. Even the most gifted of natural athletes have to learn the rules, the customs, and the special techniques of their sport. When I signed my first professional contract in 1972 and went to the tryout camp, I was easily the worst catcher there. I had to learn all the special skills that the position requires.

One skill in particular that I had to learn was how to block balls. We had a special ball-blocking drill. After it, my arms were covered with bruises, and so were the insides of my legs. It would have been easy—and certainly less painful—to quit. But I wanted to play. That meant learning how to catch, and part of that was blocking balls. Robbie will have to learn just as much and work just as hard as I did.

But Robbie, like the rest of us, will have to work on his life as well. Friendship has to be earned just as much as a spot in the starting lineup. And as Robbie faces the problems of his life, he will probably call on the values and the lessons he has learned from baseball.

Ultimately, that's what the Iron Mask series and this first book in it are all about. There's a lot of baseball here, because Robbie and I—and probably you—have in common a love of the game. But Robbie's story is about trying to grow up and make the right choices. It won't be easy. But with work and a little help from his friends, he can do it.

And with some work, you can do it, too.

Prologue

The baseball hopped like a baby rabbit over the grass to Robbie Belmont in right field. It was a clean, hard single. Robbie ran forward and smoothly caught the ball. It was in his right hand, ready to throw, in no time. He hurled it to second base with all his might. The shortstop caught the ball chest-high. Everyone turned to look at the outfielder who had just pegged a perfect throw. *Maybe now they'll ask me to pitch!* Robbie thought. But no one did.

"Good arm out there!" the shortstop called, and the game resumed.

It was a beautiful fall day for a pickup game, and Robbie's team was ahead by a run. As he returned to his position, Robbie saw a car pull into the lot behind right field. Out of the car stepped Coach Gus Franklin and another man who wore dark sunglasses. The coach waved at Robbie, who waved back.

Last June, Coach Franklin had seen Robbie pitch his grade-school baseball team to victory in the league championship. That's where they first met. Now, Robbie was a freshman at Riverton High School. Gus Franklin was its varsity baseball coach. And varsity was what Robbie dreamed of making—as a starting pitcher. He could see himself mowing down upperclassmen with his smokeball and wicked slider. Spring tryouts were just a few months away, and Robbie wanted to be ready early.

The young man walking beside Coach Franklin looked familiar to Robbie. *Where have I seen this guy?* he wondered. Then, it hit him. Even the dark sunglasses couldn't hide his identity for long. It was Eddie Trent, the five-time all-star catcher for the New York Titans!

Coach Franklin and Eddie Trent walked toward the backstop behind home plate. As they got closer, the players said hello to the coach. Then, Trent took off his sunglasses to wipe them. The players froze where they stood, gaping. Finally, someone blurted, "Hey, that's—" But another cut him off. "We know, we know." In a moment, the players were milling around Trent. They strained for a closer look. That's when Coach Franklin shooed them back to their positions.

Out in right field, Robbie started pounding his fist into his glove. *I could just trot in now and ask the pitcher nicely for the ball.*

But the pitcher was smiling as if he'd just won the sweepstakes. Eddie Trent was going to take a turn at the plate. Everyone in the infield turned and started waving the outfielders to play deeper, *much* deeper. Robbie trotted back ten yards, but they still kept waving him. Ten more yards. Stop. Turn around. They were waving him deeper still, but he stood his ground.

The first pitch sailed over Eddie Trent's head. *The pitcher's nervous. Me, I pitch better when the stakes are higher*, thought Robbie. The next pitch was a little outside, but the Titan all-star catcher reached out and socked it toward Robbie.

Playing so deep, Robbie didn't hear the sound of the bat on the ball until a split second afterward. It was an electrifying sound, like the sky ripping open. Before he even knew what he was doing, Robbie had turned around and sprinted with all his might. He didn't even look at the ball yet. *Just run! Just run!* was all he thought.

Head down, he saw the brown grass, some leaves, and two pop-tops blur by. Raising his head, he saw a wood fence just fifteen yards away. Looking back over his shoulder, he caught sight of the ball. It whipped through the fall sky as Robbie's legs moved as fast as they would go. *I'm not going to get that*, he thought. *It's just out of my reach. Where's the fence? No time to check! There's the ball. It's too far beyond me. Too bad. But since I've come this far, what the hey—*

Robbie flew into a sprawling dive. Then he slid on his stomach toward the fence, ripping his sweat shirt in the process. Robbie's arm and glove strained outward while he slid. The ball slammed into his mitt, numbing his index finger instantly. *Got it! I can't believe it! Hot diggity!* he thought. He skidded to a stop.

6

Robbie missed the fence by no more than an inch. He could practically scrape his nose on it if he wanted. A group of tiny black ants were swarming over a Popsicle wrapper in front of his eyes.

Standing up, Robbie held his mitt high in the air. The ball was firmly trapped in it. Then he started waving for the infield to go deeper. The infielders laughed. People all over the ball field were whooping and clapping. *I'll throw the ball in from way out here. That'll show Coach Franklin and Eddie Trent what kind of arm I have.*

Robbie took a few running steps in and tried to throw the ball harder than usual. As his arm came around, the ball slipped off his fingers and dribbled into center field. Robbie groaned, slapping his glove against his thigh in disgust. It was the center fielder who threw the ball back to the infield.

Suddenly, he remembered Coach Franklin was known for demanding hustle. And Eddie Trent might be watching! Robbie ran back to his position. He saw Coach Franklin calling for the ball. The pitcher shrugged and tossed it to him. Coach Franklin dug a new ball out of his pocket and threw it to the pitcher. Then the coach and Eddie walked away, taking a path that would lead them past Robbie in right field.

The game resumed. Robbie tried to act as alert and full of hustle as he could. Everyone in Riverton knew that Coach Franklin was the scout who had brought Eddie Trent to the New York

Titans seven years ago. Robbie was determined to make a good impression on both men.

The two were talking as they walked. Then they stopped. Coach Franklin reached into his pocket and handed the baseball to Eddie. The Titan star wrote something on it with a pen. Then they started walking again.

Robbie could see Eddie holding up his hands as if in a batting grip. Coach Franklin said something, and Eddie changed the position of his hands. The coach nodded, and the two men were smiling as they drew closer to Robbie.

Whack!

Robbie was startled to see a fly ball coming straight at him. He had been paying more attention to the two men than to the game. But the ball was hit high and soft enough that Robbie had no trouble getting under it for the last out of the inning. This time, he made sure his throw was true.

"Hey, Robbie!" Coach Franklin was gesturing him to come over.

"Sir?" said Robbie, caught off guard for a second time.

"There's someone here who would like to congratulate you," said the coach.

Eddie Trent cocked his arm and lobbed the baseball to Robbie. "You got a lot of spirit, Robbie!"

For the first time all day, Robbie bobbled a catch. "Gosh, uh, thank you, Mr. Trent," he blurted finally. Eddie stuck out his hand and

Robbie shook it. Then the two men walked on past the fence and out into the parking lot.

Robbie looked down in his mitt at the ball. Across the scuffed white, a felt-tip pen had written, "Great catch, kid! You came to play!" And right under the message was the autograph of Eddie Trent! *Someday, maybe he'll be catching me!* thought Robbie.

Chapter One

Robbie and forty other guys from the high school sat on the gym bleachers. It was early spring, and they were waiting for Coach Franklin to begin the preseason baseball meeting.

Robbie's palms were sweating from excitement, and his stomach was making loud noises. Craning his neck, he counted four other freshmen he knew were trying out for pitcher. *The competition,* he thought. The blond senior up front wearing a gold sweat shirt—that was Eagle Wilson. He was last year's starting pitcher. With a mixture of admiration and envy, Robbie watched Eagle joke around easily with Coach Franklin.

Then Robbie's gaze fell on the hand of the quiet senior sitting next to him. Two scars jagged across the thumb, and the little finger seemed to stick out sideways too far.

"Foul tips," muttered the senior.

Robbie looked at him. He had dark eyebrows and a slightly sad smile. His other arm was wrapped in an elastic bandage from forearm to bicep. *Oh, the starting catcher. I forget his name,* thought Robbie. *Poor guy.*

"Gentlemen," Coach Franklin began, "I consider it a privilege to be standing up here in front of you. You look like a nice, decent group. I know you would never be hard on a defenseless, elderly baseball coach like myself."

Robbie laughed with the rest of them. The "elderly" Coach Franklin was, in fact, about forty-five years old and in great shape. He wore his usual half-smile, peering out from narrowed eyes like a scout scanning the horizon. When he caught sight of Robbie, his smile seemed to brighten before it passed on. *He remembers that catch I made!* Robbie thought. He could hear his heart booming like the soundtrack of a horror movie.

"Gentlemen," Coach Franklin went on, "tryouts begin in three weeks. I hope to see you all there. For those of you who've never had the pleasure of playing under me, be advised that you might be asked to run a lap or two."

The players from last year's team groaned at this. Coach Franklin's marathon conditioning sessions were well known. Even the local news media reported on them. Each practice ended with the coach giving his players the choice of running ten laps around the field or just one lap—around the entire city of Riverton.

"So I'd recommend each of you run for about half an hour to an hour, five times a week, in preparation."

Robbie and about five others opened the spiral notebooks they had brought. Robbie's was new. RIVERTON HIGH SCHOOL TIGERS was printed on the cover. Under this was a picture of the Riverton Tiger in a batting stance, crouching with a savage look on its face. At the top of the first page, Robbie had written "Baseball Notes" and underlined the words. Now he jotted underneath them: "Run ½ to 1 hour a day, 5 days a week."

"I'm glad to see there are a few of you with the good sense to take some of my words down," Coach Franklin continued. Robbie felt more relaxed when he heard this. "Taking notes is a sign of a good student, and only good students play on my ball club. If you don't get at least a C in each subject, you should be home studying. Learning how to learn, gentlemen, is what it's all about. If you do well in school, you can learn anything—even this challenging sport known as baseball.

"As you all know, high-school baseball seems to be this city's main attraction. It's because the high-school ball here is top level. In fact, the competition is fierce.

"But remember that baseball is still a game. Your schoolwork isn't. You've all heard about athletes who thought they were special and didn't have to study. Most of them ended up wishing they had another chance. This is *your* chance, gentlemen. You may not get another. Play hard, study hard. If you don't, you'll be off the team. Am I understood?"

Robbie and the other players nodded. They knew Coach Franklin wasn't kidding. Robbie remembered reading about the league championship game three years ago. Coach Franklin dropped his ace pitcher, Fred Hanlon, from the roster the day before the big game. Hanlon had received a D in algebra. The Tigers went on to lose the game.

"That's all for now. Get your gloves oiled, get in some running, and we'll see you all in three weeks."

With a clatter, everyone started leaving the bleachers. Robbie saw Coach Franklin gesturing in his direction. He stopped and was about to point to himself and say "Me?" when the guy with the battered hand said, "Right with you, Coach."

Robbie felt a hand on his arm. It belonged to Brian Webster. Because of illness, Brian had to repeat third and fifth grade in elementary school. It was in fifth grade the second time around for Brian that he and Robbie met and became best friends. Right now, Brian was wearing his usual smile, as if he were thinking of a private joke.

"Hey, Brian, who's that beat-up-looking guy going up to Coach Franklin now?"

"I'm glad you asked me, Robbie, and not someone else. That's only Mojo Johnson, the team captain!"

Robbie watched Mojo answer some question the coach had asked. "He's your catcher," he heard Brian say. "That's the guy you'll be pitching to when you're out there on the mound as the new freshman pitching sensation."

Robbie laughed, but kept looking. Eagle Wilson joined the coach in listening to Mojo. Robbie felt a surge of envy. The coach obviously respected these two older players.

"Let's go, Robbie," said Brian. "This meeting has made me want to play some ball!"

"Exactly right!" said Robbie, whirling around. They both made a beeline for the double doors under the red exit signs. As soon as they were outside, they started running for Brian's back yard. It had a real pitcher's mound and home plate.

As they ran, Robbie couldn't shake from his mind the picture of the coach, Eagle, and Mojo talking together. The coach and Eagle were leaning forward to hear what Mojo had to say. *Who's in charge there, anyway?* Robbie wondered.

Chapter Two

Two outs in the bottom of the ninth, thought Robbie. *Why does it always come down to two outs in the bottom of the ninth?* He stood on the mound sweating, despite the cool weather. *Bases loaded, the league leader in RBIs at the plate. Stay frosty! Rob, you still have a one-run lead. Just one more out. You can do it.*

"C'mon, Robbie baby, pitch that ol' fast ball in here!" called Brian, crouched behind the plate. "Make him the last batter!" Brian flashed the one-finger sign for a fast ball. Robbie waved for him to come out to the mound. "Just tell me what you want, Robbie. I don't feel like running out there again," called Brian. Robbie only waved more frantically. With a weary sigh, Brian trotted out.

"A pitcher and a catcher don't shout instructions to each other in the middle of a ball game!" said Robbie as soon as Brian arrived.

"Why'd you call me out here?"

"You have to give me trickier signals so the

runner on second can't read them and relay them to the batter."

"Okay. I'll flash two numbers. Multiply the first one by five, and divide by twelve."

"Ha-ha."

"How about if you subtract one from whatever I flash?"

"So if you flash two, that means one?"

"Robbie, have you been studying math behind my back?"

"I just want to do everything right, Brian!"

"What's with 'right'? Let's do it perfect!" shouted Brian, who dashed back behind home plate. "Strike this guy out on three pitches, Robbo!" he called. Brian squatted and flashed two fingers.

Two minus one means fast ball, thought Robbie. *Check the runners—that guy on third is a little too frisky. I'll stare him into a shorter lead.*

Robbie glared over at the neighbor's bushes for what seemed like an unusually long time. It was getting dark in Brian's back yard, and this two-hour fantasy game had to end soon. Brian, crouched behind the plate, couldn't always follow Robbie's highly active baseball imagination. But as far as he knew, the situation now was something like this: World Series, Titans one run ahead of the Los Angeles Lions, bases loaded, two outs in the ninth. Robbie Belmont was pitching, and Scott Newhouse (batting .341 this year) was at bat.

On the mound, Robbie was thinking, *Now I'll*

start my wind-up, smooth, relaxed, fluid, strong—

But what Brian saw from behind home plate was a choppy, compact wind-up. Then, with a sudden jolt of fury, Robbie whipped an overhand fast ball straight through the heart of the plate.

"STEE-RIKE!" called Brian. "What's the matter, Scott, too fast for you?" In a horrible imitation of the slugger's voice, Brian answered himself. "He is fast, I'll give him that. But if he throws it down the pike again, I'll smack the sucker into the middle of next week!" Chuckling to himself, Brian threw the ball back to Robbie.

Ahead of the batter! thought Robbie, as he caught Brian's toss. *The most important pitch is the first one. Get a strike, and you have the advantage. Get a ball, and the batter can't be tempted as easily into swinging at a bad pitch.*

Brian flashed two fingers again for another fast ball. Brian wasn't usually very good at catching balls thrown real hard. But for some reason, he had no trouble catching his friend's smokers.

Robbie shook off the signal for the fast ball as well as the curve. He wanted the signal for the slider, his "hope" pitch.

Brian was the one who had caught Robbie's famous "birthday slider." Eight months ago, on his fourteenth birthday, Robbie was shown how to throw the pitch by his uncle. Robbie then tried it out with Brian. It was amazing! At the last moment, the ball suddenly zigged about four inches to the side. Brian wasn't quite sure how

18

he managed to catch it, but he did. Everybody gasped and bugged their eyes and said things like "Wow! Did you see that break?"

But it never broke again. Robbie had been trying it ever since. Never again did his slider slide the tiniest bit. And now he wanted to throw his "hope" pitch against Scott Newhouse?

Brian looked at his friend against the twilight sky. Then he flashed an opened hand.

Five minus one makes four. That means SLIDER, my meanest, most amazing kill-ball! Good call, Brian! Check the runners, take my smooth, flowing wind-up, and at the last moment snap my two fingers over the ball—

Robbie grunted and the pitch shot low and way outside. It was impossible for Brian to field. It even went past the huge piece of plywood they used for a makeshift backstop.

"Wild pitch!" yelled Brian, chasing after the ball. "Tying run scores from third!" he yelled as the ball rolled onto the driveway. "Second runner trying to score from second!" he yelled when he finally picked up the ball just before it reached the street. He heaved the ball toward Robbie, standing at the plate, about two hundred feet away. But he threw it so high that it got tangled in the branches of the tree by the garage.

Brian raced over and picked up the ball, yelling, "But the runner tripped over the third-base bag and is lying stunned in the base path. Wait! Now he's getting up and running home!" Brian heaved the ball once again toward Robbie, now only about a hundred feet away.

19

Brian really didn't have a very good throwing arm. The ball drifted wide and bounced about ten times before dribbling into Robbie's glove.

"And Los Angeles wins the World Series because of a wild pitch and a throwing error on the catcher!" shouted Robbie in a mournful voice.

"Wait'll next year," said Brian, walking up to Robbie. "And in our case, that'll be tomorrow right after school."

"You know, Brian, even though my slider was a wild pitch, I thought I saw it break a lot right before it hit the dirt. It really did!"

"I don't think so, Rob. Sorry, it was just your usual straight ball."

"Are you sure?"

"Yeah."

Robbie sighed and stared at the darkening sky. "I have to get that slider working again! With that pitch, I bet I could beat out Eagle Wilson!"

They stood together a moment quietly. Brian could see the first star appear in the sky.

"You know what I'm going to do?" said Robbie. "After dinner, I'm going to the library to see if they have any pitching books."

"Pitching books?"

"Sure. The library has books about everything, right? So it should have some book that tells you how to throw a slider."

"Could be. It's worth a try, I guess."

Chapter Three

Robbie was surprised to see Eagle Wilson, Mojo Johnson, and other older players studying at the library's long tables. *Team sure has a lot of eggheads*, he thought.

Robbie's report card always made his parents shake their heads sadly, as if they were looking at a phone bill that was much higher than they expected. Almost every report card Robbie could remember mentioned "he doesn't work up to full potential." The reason, he knew, was simple: He spent as many of his waking hours as he could either playing or thinking about sports. As far as he was concerned, there were three seasons, not four: football, basketball, and baseball, his favorite. He knew where the library was only because he came in from time to time to read the sports magazines. But this time, he was going to look for a book, and he wasn't quite sure where to start.

A girl studying next to Eagle got up and walked in Robbie's direction. As she came closer, Robbie saw she was very pretty. He blushed and turned his head away. Then he heard a soft voice speak to him.

"You look like you're wondering how to find a certain book."

Robbie turned his head back. He was now looking into the face of the girl. She had smooth skin, lovely brown hair, and sparkling brown eyes. Her smile was dazzling, making her look even prettier. Robbie groped for words. "Uh, how did you know I was wondering how to find a certain book?"

"Well, you *looked* like you were looking for something, and this *is* a library. I also read minds a little. Everyone does, I think, but not everyone knows it. What kind of book are you looking for? Something to do with sports?"

Robbie stepped back in surprise. *She really can read minds,* he thought.

The girl laughed. "I guessed right, I see. I'm Cynthia Wu. And you're . . ."

"Robbie Belmont."

"What kind of sports book are you looking for, Robbie?"

"Baseball. About pitching."

Cynthia turned and ran her finger down a list taped to the side of a book rack. When her finger stopped, she whispered, "Amusement and Recreation, 700–799." She walked quickly across the floor with Robbie trailing behind her. Eagle Wilson still hadn't lifted his head, but Robbie saw that Mojo was watching him with a little smile on his face. He seemed to nod as their eyes met, but Robbie wasn't sure. By the time he caught up with Cynthia, she had two books in her hand and was pulling out a third. "No, this is about hitting," she said. "Do you want one about hitting?"

"Hitting? No, I hit okay." As he said this, a look of confidence came over his face. He wasn't aware of it, but Cynthia noticed.

"I'll bet you do. Here you are, then," she said, handing him two books. "That's all the pitching books in this library tonight!"

Robbie looked at the titles. One was *The Six Basic Pitches*. The other was *Fast-Pitch Softball—A Brief History*. He hurriedly checked the table of contents for *The Six Basic Pitches*. When he saw "Chapter 3, The Slider," he cried "All right!" before he realized he was in a library. He clapped the book shut over his mouth, and Cynthia covered her mouth to stop from laughing.

"Thanks, Cynthia. It was nice of you to help me."

"You're welcome. Nice meeting you," she said. She walked back to her chair next to Eagle, who was still buried in a book.

Robbie put the softball book back on the shelf. Then he got in line to check out *The Six Basic Pitches*. Mojo got in line behind him.

"Studying hard, kid?"

"Yeah, on my pitching," said Robbie. He held up the book so Mojo could read the title.

"I meant studying as in homework. You get good grades?"

23

"Cs, except for a D-plus in math."

Mojo shook his head. "That means you have three weeks to earn a note from your math teacher saying you're doing C work this quarter."

"I know, I know," said Robbie, shrugging his shoulders. "I'll just have to work harder, I guess."

"You guess?" said Mojo. "Look, kid, why do you think Eagle and the guys are in the library now? Didn't you hear what the coach said?"

"I heard. I'll get it up to a C . . . somehow."

"You better. Otherwise, no baseball." Mojo clapped Robbie softly on the shoulder. "Get a tutor. Something. Anything. If you want to play, that is."

Robbie felt as if he'd been hit in the stomach.

That night, home in his room, Robbie sat at his desk with two books in front of him. His fingers were itching to open the pitching book to the chapter on the slider. But the thought of how much math he had to learn in three weeks had him in a panic now. Suddenly, he thought, *Melinda Clark! She's a math wiz. She can help me. I'll ask her tomorrow.*

In two seconds, Robbie had the pitching book open to chapter three and was reading away. He read the slider chapter four straight times. He studied each sentence carefully, trying out various grips and new motions with one of the three baseballs he always kept on his desk. His parents were pleasantly surprised when they stopped at his doorway to say good night. Robbie was studying, really studying! They couldn't see that it was a sports book, not a school book.

By eleven o'clock, Robbie had added a few changes to his slider technique. Robbie got up from his desk and began throwing his new pitch softly into his pillow. *Not bad*, he thought.

Then, seeing how late it was, Robbie put the baseball back on his desk. He switched off the light and jumped into bed. *Not bad at all*, he thought, drifting off to sleep.

Chapter Four

Robbie took his pitching book to school the next day. He reviewed the slider chapter whenever he could. Only in math class did he put the book aside and try to pay more attention than usual. But the more attention he paid, the more he realized he barely knew what the teacher was talking about. He grew so worried about whether he'd be able to try out for the team, he even stopped thinking about his slider. At the bell, Robbie asked his teacher what he'd have to do to earn a C average before tryouts. "Get a B on the midterm exam in two weeks," the teacher replied.

After school, he found his friend Melinda Clark by her locker. Robbie explained his math-baseball problem. Melinda lived two houses down the street from Robbie. They grew up together, played video games, rode skateboards, and even sat around doing nothing together on an occasional summer afternoon.

"So what do you say, Melinda? Can you help me learn the math I need? I'll do anything for you in return. Just name it."

Melinda looked at Robbie for a long time. She wondered if he'd stick with it. Finally, she said, "Okay. I'll come over tonight around eight. Try not to lose your mind in the meantime."

"Ha-ha! Great! Eight o'clock it is! Thanks, Melinda! See you then!" With that, Robbie dashed away. He had a date with destiny in Brian's back yard.

Brian wasn't there yet when Robbie arrived. This wasn't surprising, since Robbie had run the whole way. Robbie jerked an almost-new baseball from his book bag, dropped the book bag on the ground, shoved the large bounce-back net behind the plate, and trotted to the mound.

At last! He tossed an easy pitch, not his slider, to test the net. The ball sprung back at him in a soft line. *Perfect! All right! Now's the time.* He stood there a moment, recalling all the new things he had learned about slider pitching. Then he wound up and fired.

The pitch broke like crazy. Hitting the net, it bounced back wide of Robbie's reach. But he just stood there gaping. Finally, he went to retrieve the ball from the back bushes. From there, he threw another slider in the general direction of the bounce-back net.

The longer throw showed the slider breaking even more. It broke so far that it missed the bounce-back net *and* the plywood backstop. The ball bounced merrily toward the driveway. Just at that moment, Brian appeared. He fielded the ball neatly without breaking stride.

"Hey, Rob!" he said as he trotted up. "Have you cracked the secret of the slider yet? Get out there on that mound and bend that ball in to me!" Brian already had his glove on. He went right behind the plate into a catcher's crouch.

Robbie walked slowly to the mound and took his pitching position. He stood there smiling.

"What are you grinning at, goofball? Throw the pitch, would you? Let's see what all that book learning's done for you!"

Robbie felt the weight of the ball at his fingertips. He slid his fingers together off the ball's center, feeling for the scratchy seam. He didn't bother with the wind-up, though he decided to throw more sidearm than usual. Again, the slider broke like a dream. *That's just what it is—a dream come true!*

Brian was startled by the ball's sudden break. He just barely managed to snag it by lurching wildly at the last split second. "Wow!" he yelled. Brian stood up, put his hands on his hips, and grinned at Robbie. "Now *that* is what I call a *slider*! It broke a *ton*, Robbie."

"I know ... I know," said Robbie. He still couldn't believe it.

"C'mon, throw it twice in a row, and maybe we'll see your face on a bubble-gum card someday!" said Brian. He tossed the ball back to Robbie.

The next pitch was also a picture-perfect slider, and Brian caught it with a whoop. Then he lofted it above his head and started doing a weird dance around home plate. As he did,

Brian chanted, "Slider, slider, slider, slider!" Robbie wasn't exactly sure why he found Brian's dance so funny. But he was laughing just the same.

Before nightfall ended their session, Robbie had thrown over a hundred fine-snapping sliders. He couldn't remember the last time he felt so happy. It seemed he could make that baseball do anything he wanted.

When Melinda dropped over Robbie's house that night, she expected he'd be in the same bad study mood as usual. But what she found instead was someone with a determined look in his eyes. They went into the kitchen to study. As they plunged into the math, however, Melinda saw Robbie's determination slowly slip away. He was frustrated at how slowly he was learning. An hour into the lesson, Melinda was startled when Robbie slammed a fist against the kitchen table. That's when she got up and fixed herself a glass of water. Drinking it at the sink, she heard him growl behind her. "My brain wasn't meant for studying."

"Nonsense, Robbie. Everyone can study."

"Oh, yeah?"

"Yeah. Now let's get back to work."

"The worst thing is, I finally got this pitch to work today that I've been trying to get to work for *ages*."

"What did you do differently?"

"All sorts of things—finger placement, arm and

wrist motion. I found a book on it in the library, and I read—"

"Aha!" shouted Melinda, interrupting. She wagged a finger at Robbie. "You *studied*! See, you *can* study! If you can do it for baseball, you can darn well do it for math! Because if you don't, Robbie, there's no finger placement, no arm motion, no wrist motion, no sacrifice infield fly tag-up double-play bunt, no pitcher's pen or bull mound or whatever they're called! Because there's no baseball, am I right?"

Robbie knew she was right, even if she didn't know beans about baseball.

Chapter Five

First day of tryouts! thought Robbie. *At last!*

Riverton High School's baseball field was alive with the chatter of forty or more boys. They were throwing balls back and forth to loosen up a bit. Robbie was tossing with Brian, taking it easy as the coach had warned, not trying to throw his slider. *My arm's in good shape,* thought Robbie, *because of all the pitching practice I've been doing.* Still, he felt a slight tightness right above his elbow.

Robbie was also a little tired. He'd had weeks of intense tutoring from Melinda. She made him study math as hard as he studied the slider chapter. Robbie then took the midterm exam. When he got it back, a large B in red ink was circled on the front.

Never before had he done such hard mental work for such a long stretch of time. It could be as exhausting as weightlifting, he was surprised to learn. But it also seemed to make him more aware. He seemed to notice all sorts of things he never noticed before. He noticed the tiny hitch in Eagle Wilson's pitching motion right before his arm moved forward. He could see Mojo Johnson wince ever so slightly as he tried out his arm for the first time since his winter finger operation. Robbie could also tell who was confident and who wasn't. And through it all, he was aware of Coach Franklin weaving in and around the ball field, watching everything. Robbie felt great.

Then the conditioning began. First, there was calisthenics. It began with slow laps. That wasn't so bad. Sprints came next. *Uh-oh*, thought Robbie. They sprinted ten yards at first and walked ten. Then they sprinted twenty yards and walked ten. Soon, they were running fifty yards and jogging ten.

By the time the sprints ended, Robbie and the other boys were hunched over and panting for breath. Coach Franklin told them to walk around with their hands over their heads for a minute. "You'll get more oxygen that way," he explained. They did as they were instructed.

It seemed as if only ten seconds went by before the coach spoke again. "Minute's up, gentlemen!"

Brian, red in the face, looked over at Robbie. "He's got to be kidding!" Brian whispered to Robbie.

"I don't think so," answered Robbie between breaths.

"Now that we've loosened our limbs a little, gentlemen, I thought we'd run a few races. Just a few." Those last words from the coach brought some groans from the boys.

"Think he means a few hundred or a few thousand, Rob?" asked Brian softly.

Before Robbie could reply, Coach Franklin started dividing the boys up in different groups for racing. On his grade-school teams, Robbie had always been the fastest. But after watching some races, even after winning his first two heats, he wasn't so sure. Another guy had won all his heats, too. In fact, the heats he ran weren't even close. He'd be crossing the finish line of a fifty-yard dash as the other runners reached the half-way point. Brian was in one of those heats with him.

"I'm telling you, Rob, that guy has rockets in his sneakers. I saw nothing but his heels the whole race."

Soon, word was whispered around that the guy had just moved from South Carolina and was an Olympic track hopeful.

The next heat pitted Robbie against him. Robbie was determined to make a good showing. The coach said "Ready, set, go!" and the boys bolted forward. Robbie churned ahead of the other guys. Ten yards, twenty yards passed. Then he glanced sideways. All the guys were behind Robbie—except one. *Who is this guy?* wondered Robbie, a good ten yards behind him. Try as he did, Robbie couldn't make up the ground between them. He lost by fifteen yards.

That was the closest anyone had come to beating the guy.

Robbie was still out of breath when he walked over to the winner and stuck out his hand. "Nice race. I'm Robbie Belmont."

"I'm Ralph Butler."

Robbie was still panting as they shook hands. That's when Robbie noticed Ralph Butler was breathing no harder than if he had been cutting the lawn on a sit-down mower.

"You sure run fast, Ralph."

"I do a lot of track."

"What position are you going out for?"

"Whatever one the coach thinks I'll be good at."

Robbie was about to ask another question when Coach Franklin called for quiet. "Everyone from last year's team report to the batting cage," he shouted. "All others follow me."

The coach headed toward the opposite end of the field. Robbie and a number of other boys walked behind him. Looking over his shoulder, Robbie felt his heart sink. He saw Mojo warming up Eagle and two other pitchers from last year's team near the batting cage. *That's where I should be!*

Coach Franklin ran some fielding drills. He chopped a grounder to a player, who threw it to another player covering first base. The process was repeated for each boy. Brian Webster managed to field his first try, though clumsily. His throw bounced twice getting to the first baseman.

"What a wimp!"

Robbie turned around and glared at the speaker. He was a lanky blond kid with a sneer on his face. "What are you staring at, Big Boy?" the kid asked.

Robbie kept glaring. None of the things that crossed his mind just then seemed worth saying. He turned back around. *Not a guy to trust,* he concluded.

Robbie watched the guy in front of him smoothly pick up a four-bouncer and fire a strike to first base. *My turn!*

Robbie got into a hunched, loose-kneed fielding position. Coach Franklin shouted, "All right now, kid!" and hit a stinging liner that streaked at Robbie's feet. Instinctively, Robbie took a small step forward and lowered his glove. He never took his eyes off the ball. It bounced immediately into the webbing of his glove. As Robbie pivoted, his long, strong fingers wrapped the ball firmly. He cocked the ball behind his ear and pegged it toward first base. Robbie had done all this in one, smooth motion.

"Hey, kid," shouted Coach Franklin, "take another. Let me hit you a real ground ball. Here you go! Dang!"

Again, it was a low, hard line drive. But this time, it was hit sharply to Robbie's right. He backhanded the ball and made another good throw to first base.

"Sorry, son," the coach called. "Let me try that again!"

This time, the liner bounced right in front of Robbie. He made a short-hop pickup and threw the ball to first.

Coach Franklin hit five more like that at Robbie. Each time, he'd chime out, "Sorry! Dang it! Try it again, kid!" The whole team was enjoying the coach's show. Robbie was backhanding, charging, scooping, and spearing the hit balls without fail. All his throws were dead on. He was smiling a little, enjoying himself. Still, he wondered why the coach was doing this to him.

Finally, Coach Franklin hit Robbie a sizzling three-bouncer that sent him five yards to the left. He barely snagged it on a high bounce, and he threw it off balance while running. The throw kicked up dust in front of the first baseman, who couldn't make the catch. "My fault," Robbie said to the first baseman. "Sorry."

Next was the blond-haired guy who had made the insulting remark about Brian Webster. Coach Franklin also sent him a short hopper, which he fielded without a problem.

Ralph Butler then took his turn fielding. Robbie was surprised by what he saw. Ralph didn't seem to know the first thing about ground balls. He missed four of the five hit to him. And his throws weren't very accurate.

Coach Franklin closely watched every boy taking a ground ball from him. Though he never made it to the major leagues, the coach had played some minor-league ball. He had also done a little scouting in the past for the pros. That's how he first saw Eddie Trent, a great raw talent then. It was Coach Franklin who brought Eddie to the attention of the New York Titans. He knew talent, *real* talent, when he saw it. And he saw it in Robbie Belmont.

Robbie, however, didn't notice. His attention kept drifting to the pitchers and Mojo. They were throwing harder now. *But none of them seem to have many breaking pitches. No slider, that much I can see! I may have a chance at starting pitcher yet!*

But Robbie didn't get a chance to show his pitching stuff that day. After the ground-ball drill, Coach Franklin called for final laps. After ten, he called "Just one more!" He said this *five more times,* and everyone was counting. Finally, the first day of tryouts was over. "Whew!" gasped Robbie as he trotted off the field with the other boys.

Chapter Six

The sun was high in the sky the next day. Tryouts for Riverton High School's baseball team continued. The smack of ball meeting glove could be heard all over the field. Robbie knew he'd get a chance to pitch today. Coach Franklin said he'd try each new player at every position.

After a shorter version of the previous day's conditioning drills, the coach called for batting practice. While the players took their allotted number of hits (five), Coach Franklin hit fly balls to others in the outfield. Robbie caught a few of the towering fly balls himself. The coach would hit one their way and five guys would yell "Mine!" or "I got it!" Then three guys would repeat the claim, then two, then two again (louder), until finally, one lone call claimed the fly ball. Sometimes, the ball dropped into dueling gloves of two different players.

Robbie was called in to take his turn hitting. He picked out a bat that felt comfortable in his hands and walked to the plate. *Pow!* In one compact swing, he sent the first pitch sailing out into center field. *Whack!* This time, he knocked a home run high over the left fielder's head. *Bam!* It was a screecher through the middle, just missing the head of the batting practice pitcher. *Crack!* Robbie sent a shot down the third-base line, a sure triple. *Boom!* This last hit was a monster. The ball seemed to be still rising as it flew over the fence in deep center field.

The eyes of all the players on the field were on Robbie as he walked away from the batting cage. Even Coach Franklin stood there staring.

Brian and Ralph batted poorly. The insulting blond-haired kid hit well, spraying line drives in the outfield. José Sanchez, last year's leading batter, hit even more impressively than Robbie had. And that was saying a lot! Mojo hit carefully but solidly. Eagle, Robbie was quick to notice, only hit two soft singles and three dribbling grounders. *Pitchers don't need to hit that well*, he thought. *But it never hurts!*

After batting practice, Coach Franklin set up a new fielding drill for the new players. They would rotate through all the positions. Robbie started out in right field. That meant he had to wait until the coach hit balls to every other position. *The right fielder is always last.*

Finally, Coach Franklin tagged an awesome fly in Robbie's direction. It forced Robbie to run back as he had when he caught Eddie Trent's hit. This time, he didn't have to dive for the ball. Robbie caught it over his shoulder while running full tilt. His throw to the relay was right on the mark.

Coach Franklin blew his whistle, and the fielders rotated to the next position. Robbie trotted to center field, the most spacious baseball position of all. It was the outfield's control headquarters. The coach hit one between him and Brian, who was in left field. Brian had a better chance at the ball, though he wasn't calling for it. So Robbie called "Yours!" and veered off. Brian arrived under the ball with plenty of time, but the ball squibbed out of his mitt. He had tried to throw it before he caught it. Brian ran back into position without any display of temper. But Robbie knew he was mad at himself.

Then Coach Franklin blooped the ball into short center field. It looked as if the ball would fall exactly between three fielders. Robbie, the second baseman, and the shortstop were all sprinting toward the same spot. It was Robbie's job to call who would catch it, but he had to wait a few more split seconds to tell. He could hear the thumping footsteps getting closer.

Finally, when he knew he could catch it, Robbie yelled "Mine!" The two infielders crisscrossed, sidestepping each other to avoid a bone-crunching crash. Robbie kept on chugging and caught the ball at his shoe tips. Then he made a clothesline throw to the guy playing catcher. "Good call!" Coach Franklin sang out. Robbie thought it odd that the coach said "Good call!" instead of "Good catch!" or "Good throw!"

The next whistle sent Robbie to left field. It was the busiest position in the outfield because of all the hits by right-handed batters. Sure enough, the coach gave him plenty to do. Calling

"Home, Robbie!" he whacked a liner down the third-base line. Robbie dashed right and snagged the skittering bouncer. Slamming down his right foot, Robbie pivoted and flung the ball home. But the throw was off the mark, staying outside the foul line. *I should have gotten better balance before I threw*, Robbie thought, running back into position with his head down.

Next came third base, "the hot corner." A third baseman barely had time to think and rarely needed more than two steps to make a fast-breaking fielding play. Coach Franklin hit a hard hopper over the third-base bag. Robbie took two steps. The ball smacked into his mitt. He stopped, took a moment to get balanced, and whipped a perfect throw to first. "Nice peg, kid!" called the coach. *That's a long throw*, thought Robbie. *It's as long as the catcher's throw to second base.*

Shortstop is the land where the best fielders range. It's the position that makes the most fielding plays. A consistent shortstop usually saves about three runs a game. Master of hops and pops, he has to go in any direction, and throw from balanced and unbalanced stances. He also has to be so sure-handed that the whole team feels confident when the hit goes to him.

Robbie was a fast, quick-handed fielder. But he found he couldn't quite reach two grounders the coach poked through the holes over second base and between him and the third baseman. "Sorry, Robbie," Coach Franklin called. Then he drilled a third grounder right at him. Robbie gloved it easily and fired a frustrated sizzler to first.

Robbie now moved to second base. He thought, *In the outfield, you had time to think when fielding. Infield is almost all reflex.* When the coach called "Get two!" and hit the ball down the middle, Robbie didn't hesitate. He streaked right and snatched the ball. This left him in a cramped, scrunched position going away from his target.

Still, Robbie managed to flip the ball from somewhere under his knee to the shortstop covering second base. The shortstop caught it barehanded and made the double-play throw to Brian at first base. *No way to plan a flip toss like that,* Robbie mused. *You just have to let yourself go with the action!* "Way to look, Bri!" Robbie called to his friend.

When Robbie moved to first base, he had no trouble receiving all the throws from the infielders. *This must be a lot like catching,* he thought, *except everyone throws you only fast balls.* There were no runners during these fielding drills. But Robbie still took care to place his foot on the inner edge of the bag as he stretched to catch the throws. A misplaced foot or a bad throw could lead to a collision with the batter racing to first.

Robbie found himself comparing this position to catching, too. *Catchers have collisions with runners intent on scoring. Only catchers don't avoid collisions. They have to block the plate and catch the throw at the same time!*

Coach Franklin blew his whistle, and Robbie hustled toward home plate to try his hand at catching. The ever-cheery coach was standing there holding a bat in one hand. His other hand held out to Robbie a catcher's mitt.

"I like the way you hustle, Robbie," said the coach. "Now let's see what you can do behind the plate."

"Thank you, sir. Pitching's what I really do best."

"Well, we'll see. Right now, you're the catcher. It's a hard job, you know, but it's where all the action is. Get one!"

With that, Coach Franklin hit the third baseman a grounder. He threw to first, and the first baseman threw to Robbie. He reached up and the ball zoomed into the catcher's mitt. To Robbie's surprise, the mitt wrapped snugly around the ball with hardly any effort on his part. *It's like a ball-eating hand pillow!* he thought.

The coach took the ball from Robbie and slapped a grounder to Ralph Butler at shortstop. It went right between Ralph's legs. "That's all right, Ralph! Try another!" Coach Franklin hit a perfectly placed two-hopper that Ralph only had to lift his glove a bit to field. But he flubbed the catch.

As Ralph chased down the ball he muffed, the coach turned to Robbie at home plate. "I've been coaching baseball for fifteen years, Robbie, and I've never seen an athlete faster than Ralph there. I just don't think he played much baseball when he was growing up. He doesn't react to the ball the way you and some of the others do."

Robbie found himself quietly excited by Coach Franklin's private remarks to him. He never realized before that the catcher is the only player

43

next to the coach during infield practice. The catcher hears what the coach thinks out loud. He shares the coach's view in a way. They were the only two facing all the others on the field. *No wonder Mojo and the coach speak so easily and freely with each other,* thought Robbie. *It's good for me to realize this. As a pitcher, I'll be working with a catcher all the time.*

Coach Franklin grounded a ball to second, second threw to first, and first threw to Robbie. Robbie caught the ball and pegged it right to the second-base bag.

"Way to go, Robbie," said the coach. "Even with a good lead, a base stealer would have to be pretty fast to beat a throw like that." Coach Franklin now looked directly at him. "But then, bases aren't just stolen on the catcher—they're stolen on the pitcher, too. If a pitcher's delivery from the stretch is too long, *pffft!* That runner is sliding safely into the bag."

Robbie nodded. "I see what you mean, Coach." Zipping that ball to where the second baseman could make an easy tag on a base stealer made Robbie feel good.

Coach Franklin hit one to the guy playing first, who ran to the bag, stepped on it, and sent in a bad throw at Robbie's feet. But Robbie scooped up the ball easily. *Mr. Pillow just gobbles those short hoppers like popcorn!* Robbie tossed the ball gently to the coach.

Rather than catching it, Coach Franklin slapped the ball with his hand a few feet in front of the plate. The ball slapping was his way of laying down a bunt that the catcher has to field. Robbie pounced on it. He barehanded it cleanly and powered a throw to first.

"Right idea, Robbie," said the coach. "Wrong location. You just threw the ball at the batter's back. Next time, keep your throw a bit more inside the base path. You want to throw him out, not bean him from behind."

Coach Franklin slapped another fake bunt. This time, Robbie fielded and threw the ball perfectly.

The coach gave the infielders double-play drills. All the while, he made frequent comments to Robbie. Then Coach Franklin sent flies and base hits to the outfielders, and they threw to second, third, and home.

On the throws home, the first baseman stationed himself on a line with a throw. Robbie was supposed to yell "Cut!" if the throw looked off the mark. This gave the first baseman more time to prevent runners from advancing. If the throw looked good, Robbie was supposed to say nothing. The first baseman would then let the ball pass. Coach Franklin agreed with every decision Robbie made.

Then the coach blew the whistle for the next rotation. "Good work, Robbie!" he said. "You go over there with Mojo now and take your turn pitching. I'll catch you later."

"Thanks, Coach."

At last! At last! At last! Robbie ran eagerly toward the practice mound outside the right-field line.

Now I'll show 'em!

Chapter Seven

Robbie stood on the mound sweating. Mojo Johnson didn't look particularly impressed yet by Robbie's pitching. He had called out "Good speed, kid!" at one point. It made Robbie smile, although he was hoping to hear something like "*Great* speed, kid!" A little later, Mojo had called out again. "Is your arm sore at all, stiff maybe?" Robbie had answered no. He didn't think the tiny twinge above his elbow was worth mentioning.

Robbie powered in his fastest fast ball yet. It whomped into Mojo's mitt loud enough to make a few heads turn from the playing field. Mojo, looking puzzled, walked out to Robbie.

"How are you gripping that fast ball of yours?" he asked, handing Robbie the ball.

"The standard way." Robbie held the ball out and showed each grip as he explained. "You know, across the seams for it to lift, and with the seams for it to sail out."

"Okay. Just curious. Those are the right grips. I just don't know why your fast ball doesn't *dance*. Let me see your curve next." Mojo trotted back into position. "Go easy at first. Take about five pitches to get up to full speed."

After the fourth curve, Mojo called out to Robbie, "Okay, give it all you got."

Robbie did. But the curve still didn't have much zip or break.

"Well, Robbie," Mojo said, "we'll call that pitch a slurve. That's a slow curve—if that."

"I know I don't have a curve, Mojo. The slider is my best pitch. Besides my fast ball."

"Oh! Let's see your slider then."

This is it! Robbie's fingers gripped the ball for a slider. He went right into his motion confidently. This was a pitch he had thrown so much recently that his body performed with grooved confidence. The pitch veered nicely right over the low outside corner. *Another slider strike!* he thought. *How did you like that, Mojo?*

Mojo tossed the ball back and called, "That's it. You threw it nice and easy. Now let's see you throw it full speed."

Full speed? I put everything I had on that pitch! Robbie thought. Mojo clearly wasn't impressed.

Robbie turned around, took off his glove, and rubbed the ball with both hands. He felt every inch of it. "C'mon, Belmont," he muttered to himself. "Concentrate!"

Robbie put on his glove, turned around, and looked at the target Mojo was giving him. He was determined to throw the best slider he had in him. Robbie went into his wind-up and fired. The slider broke more sharply than ever. But

Mojo just tossed the ball back, saying nothing. Robbie hurled three more sliders with the same fierce concentration. Each seemed better than the one before! Mojo never said a word until after the fifth one.

"Okay, let's see your change-up now."

With a hollow feeling in his stomach, Robbie threw five change-ups. He knew his change-up was nothing special, just a slower speed. *Why doesn't he say anything about my slider?*

At this point, Coach Franklin came over. "How's the kid doing on the mound, Mojo?"

"Have a look, Coach." Coach Franklin took a position like an umpire's behind Mojo. "Robbie," called out Mojo, "go through all your pitches for the coach."

Robbie began with his fast ball. The hard *thwap* into Mojo's mitt made the coach's eyes open wide. Then Robbie threw his curve, change-up, and slider. He saved the slider for last. Robbie hoped to catch the coach by surprise with it. But he just stood there, barely blinking, as the pitches came in.

Coach Franklin and Mojo spoke a while quietly. Then both of them came toward the mound. *Why do they look so serious?* wondered Robbie.

"Tell him what you saw, Mojo," said the coach.

"Well, Robbie, your fast ball is very fast. But it's not lively. That makes it easy to hit. Even you know your curve and change-up are not your best pitches. That leaves your slider." Here Robbie brightened, waiting to hear some sort of compliment. "Well, it's okay, but that's about all. It could fool a few batters. But it's still not enough to offset the straightness of your fast ball."

"Wait a minute. I think it'll fool a lot more than a few batters." Robbie felt his sweat grow cold up and down his back.

"Well now, Robbie," said the coach, shaking his head very slowly, "a slider's the easiest breaking ball to hit. Let me show you something. Take Mojo's mitt here, and I'll throw you a slider. Go ahead now. Hustle."

Robbie took the catcher's mitt from Mojo and hustled behind home plate. He fell into a natural catcher's squat. This made Mojo and the coach exchange glances and smiles.

"Okay, Robbie, here comes a slider."

Coach Franklin wound up and flung a slider that broke half a foot more than Robbie's. "Whoa!" Robbie said out loud as he caught the pitch. On one knee, he lobbed the ball back to the coach. "That was amazing, Coach!"

"If it was so amazing, how come you caught it so easily?"

Robbie froze. Then he said, "Well, I knew it was coming. And I guess I catch well."

"Come on back out here, Robbie," said the coach from the mound. Robbie ambled out. "Yes, you knew the slider was coming, and you do catch well. But that's not the point. The slider stays on the same plane. For it to be effective, it has to break a lot and it has to come as a surprise to the batter. Your slider, Robbie, doesn't break much. And since your curve and change-up are soft, the only pitch left is that straight fast ball of yours. It's hard to win games on just two pitches, especially when they don't have much motion on them. Understand?"

"But I'm just starting to get my slider working, Coach. It's still developing."

Coach Franklin took his hand and gently squeezed Robbie's right elbow. Robbie winced. It felt like fire flashing up his arm. The coach released his grip and looked at Robbie.

"Mojo told me you might have some stiffness in that right arm of yours," the coach said. "Seems he was right. The slider puts a tremendous strain on the arm, especially a young arm. And you've got an early case of slider elbow, Robbie. If it worsens, it could ruin your baseball career. No more sliders, okay? At least until your elbow heals completely."

Robbie nodded. He felt he couldn't speak. A lump formed in his throat. He hated the quiet, serious look Mojo was giving him. He felt like he wanted to scream "You're blind!" to the coach and run off the field.

"Think about it, Robbie," the coach added. "Think about what position would best use your talents. Now, let's finish this practice."

Coach Franklin blew his whistle and called for final laps. Robbie ran around and around in a daze. He barely noticed how hard he was panting and how his legs ached. *No slider?* he kept thinking. *Does that mean no pitching?*

In the locker room after practice, he got dressed without a word as the other players kidded around. The blond-haired kid, it turned out, thought snapping wet towels at people was the height of humor. When Robbie saw him start to aim one at Brian, he grabbed the towel away.

"Ah, if it isn't Big Boy! I'm Eddie Mosely, Big Boy. Pleased to meet you. Now give me my towel back before I make you eat it." Mosely had two sidekicks who snickered at this remark.

Robbie felt too tired to get irritated. He handed the towel back and just said, "Don't snap it at anyone again, Eddie. And my name is Robbie, not Big Boy."

"I'll try to remember all that, Big Boy," Eddie cackled. Then he turned to snap the towel at someone else. But Ralph Butler came up and stopped him. "What *is* your problem, Mosely? Belmont said stop, and I'm saying stop. I won't say it again."

Ralph took the towel from Mosely and ripped it in two. It came apart like a sheet of newspaper in his hands. All the time, Ralph glared at Mosely. Then Ralph handed him the two soggy pieces and said, "Next time, it'll be you. Catch my drift?"

"Uh, why, sure, Ralph. That's cool," sputtered Mosely. The muscular Butler was no one to mess with. "Hey, thanks, Ralph. I've always wanted two towels." Mosely shut his locker and scurried off with his two friends.

"Hey, Robbie," Ralph said.

"Hi, Ralph. Mr. Personality there."

"He uses his head for a darkroom, all right. How are you? You look a little down."

"Yeah." There was a pause, but Ralph didn't push it. *What the heck*, Robbie thought, *why not tell him? It can't make anything worse.* He looked at Ralph and said, "I'm a pitcher, Ralph. I've always been a pitcher, all through grade school. It's the only position I've ever wanted to play. But Mojo said a couple of things about my pitching to the coach. And now he doesn't like my pitching."

"Did Coach Franklin see you pitch?"

"Yeah, but only four pitches. I'm dead, man. Really. I can't hack this. Now he won't even let me throw my slider. Says it'll ruin my arm, even though I've been throwing it the last few months."

"How long?"

"Last few weeks, actually," said Robbie, laughing uneasily.

"Whew! That's rough, Robbie."

"Maybe I should transfer to another school. You know, one where I have a better shot at making pitcher."

"Whoa there, Robbie. That's sailing a little too far from shore, don't you think?"

"Maybe. Maybe not."

"Look, I'll tell you something. This was my last day of practice."

Robbie was stunned. But he could see Ralph was serious. "I'm not a baseball player. I know that now. I like the sport. I like how it looks. You know, all that room, the grass and the base paths and the bleachers. But I've decided. I was talking with my mom and dad about it last night. I have to concentrate on track. It's what I do best. And it's my best shot at a college scholarship. What I'm saying is, go with your strengths. If pitching isn't what you do best, it's not what you should go for."

"I don't know, Ralph. I have to do some thinking, I guess. Thanks anyway."

That night, alone in his room, Robbie was gloomy again, worse than ever. He sat at the edge of his bed. His book bag lay unopened on the floor, with his undone homework buried inside. He reached for the ball signed by Eddie Trent. It was on top of his nightstand. Robbie started tossing the ball up and down, over and over. Then he gazed out his window. All he could see was darkness.

Chapter Eight

Robbie couldn't shake off his disappointment. Very quickly, he fell into a mental slump. Bad habits returned. He did just enough homework to get by. And he skipped Melinda's tutoring sessions twice in a row.

His attitude on the baseball field wasn't much better. Robbie went through the last two days of tryouts in a fog. He loafed during conditioning exercises. All too often, he gazed blankly at the ground during drills. Sometimes he did this when Coach Franklin was explaining something. Robbie hardly talked to any of the other players. Even Brian, his best friend, could barely get a word out of him.

On the last day of tryouts, Robbie asked Coach Franklin if he could *please* have one more chance to show his pitching. The coach finally agreed. "But no sliders!" he warned.

Robbie pitched to four batters during a scrimmage game. His speed got the first batter to hit weakly for an out. But the next two knocked his fast ball for hard base hits. Frustrated, Robbie then threw a slider to José, the fourth batter. José clobbered it, sending the pitch into the school parking lot four hundred feet away.

"Nice pitching, Big Boy!" sang out Mosely, who was doing the catching. Robbie's knees were trembling. He wondered if he should run at Mosely and tackle him. Before he could decide, Coach Franklin came to the mound and pulled him firmly to the sideline. The coach was hopping mad.

"If I tell you no sliders, I *mean* no sliders," he said sternly. "Did you see my two rules on the locker-room bulletin board?"

Robbie had. So had everyone else. The coach had posted just two rules: "Rule Number One: The coach is always right. Rule Number Two: When the coach is wrong, see Rule Number One." Robbie and the others had laughed when they read them. But he wasn't laughing now, nor was the coach.

"If you want to play on this baseball team, Robbie, you'll play by my rules, by what I say. No exceptions. Understand?"

Robbie nodded meekly. He knew the coach was right.

Coach Franklin gently put his hand on Robbie's shoulder. "Is everything all right at home, Robbie?"

"Oh, fine, sir. Really." *Mom and Dad are nice,* he thought. *They always have been. I like them, and we usually get along. Just lately I've been wanting to spend most of my time by myself.*

"Okay, Robbie," the coach said. "Go relieve Mojo at first base for now. And show some life! This is a baseball field, not a hypnotist convention!"

The next day, Coach Franklin posted in the locker room a list of all those who had made the team. Robbie and Brian looked at it together. Robbie barked "Oh, no!" when he failed to find his name under PITCHERS. When he finally did find his name, he spit out, "That does it! No way do I stay at this school!" He kicked a locker and ran out of the building. He ended up leaning against a big elm tree by the parking lot.

About five awful minutes passed. Then Brian came quietly up to him. "Sorry you're so disappointed, Robbie. But I'm glad you made the team."

"Made the team? As what? A catcher! Can you believe that? A CATCHER!" He screamed the word out so loud that Cynthia Wu, just then putting her schoolbooks in Eagle's car, looked over, startled.

"Well, at least you made the team," said Brian, looking away.

"I don't want to catch! I don't want my pitching hand to get like Mojo's, all bruised and bumped."

"The new one-handed mitt will help—"

"Nuts to that thing! This is my mitt, Brian, here!" He waved his glove in Brian's face. "Catcher! You know what they call that lobster costume catchers wear? The tools of ignorance! Tools for anyone stupid enough to spend half the game squatting, grunting, mucking around in the dirt, getting knocked and whonked, while the pitcher's out there soaking in all the glory!"

"Well, Robbie, as I said, at least *you* made the team! You should be grateful! Some guys aren't as lucky as that, you know. Some guys aren't as lucky as you! Some guys are not born with speed, power, a great arm, and hitting and fielding genius! Some guys don't even get any of it!"

Brian whirled and stormed off. *Oh, no! Brian didn't make the team! Brian got cut!* Robbie suddenly realized. He started to call out "I'm sorry, Brian!" but then didn't. *The heck with it. I have my own problems.* Then he saw Cynthia Wu at the other end of the parking lot, looking in his direction with a worried expression on her face.

Robbie turned around and called, "Sorry, Brian!" Brian kept walking away without turning around, although he lifted his hand to indicate he heard. Robbie looked back across the lot, but Cynthia Wu had already left.

Robbie's parents didn't have much trouble convincing him that transferring to another school was out of the question. "You'll have to do all the phone calls, visits to other principals, and paperwork yourself, Robbie," his mother said. "I just don't have the time." And his dad said, "You'll probably have to take at least half your freshman year over again."

Melinda called him as he lay on his bed listening to a rock-and-roll radio station.

"Where are you?" she demanded on the phone.

"I have to stop the tutoring for a while, Melinda. There are too many other things on my mind these days."

"You should have called me and told me."

"Sorry."

"What's wrong?"

"I didn't make the team."

"You didn't make the team? No way, Robbie! There's no way you didn't make the team."

"I didn't make pitcher. Coach listed me as catcher. So, anyway, thanks, Melinda. I have to go."

"Robbie, don't be a dope!"

Robbie put the phone back in its cradle.

He went through the first days of team practice halfheartedly. On the third day, when Robbie was taking his turn catching for infield practice, Coach Franklin spoke to him.

"Robbie, you know why I put you at catcher, don't you?" *Whack!* The coach hit one to the second baseman. Robbie tossed a second ball to the coach.

"Not really, sir."

"It's not just because you have such a sunny disposition all the time." *Thunk!* Robbie caught a throw from Mojo at first and pegged it to second. The throw was right on the bag, though at half speed.

58

"Nice throw, Robbie, though you could have put more zip on it. You throw better from a stable position than on the run. Watch this."

Coach Franklin took another ball from Robbie and rapped what looked like a sure single down the middle. Out of nowhere appeared Luther Jones, the senior shortstop. He dashed left, cupped the ball in his glove, and flipped the ball to first base while still running hard. It was an amazing throw, right on target.

"Rabbit quickness—that's what Jonesy there has. He can get to a hole faster than anyone else in the infield. But more important, he knows what to do with the ball once he gets it. He has great balance, something that's hard to teach."

Robbie was beginning to understand what the coach meant. He was fast, but he wasn't as *quick* as Jonesy in reacting to an infield ball hit more than a couple steps away.

"On close short hoppers, Robbie, I'd rate you and Jonesy even. And a catcher gets his fair share of close short hoppers, whether from wild pitches or low fielding throws to the plate."

Robbie had already made about five of those in-the-dirt pickups since infield practice began. He'd made them so easily that he'd never thought about how crucial they could be—especially to a catcher.

Coach Franklin hit a few slow rollers now. "You know, Robbie, that fast ball of yours may not be good for pitching, but it is for catching. You can throw it straight and hard, and it goes where you want it to. You also have a quick release. Those are rare qualities ... catcher qualities."

Robbie understood what the coach was saying. And he appreciated what the coach was trying to do. But none of his remarks made Robbie feel any better. He still had his mind set on one thing—pitching. The sight of the team pitchers warming up nearby made Robbie feel only worse. By the time practice ended, he was as sad as ever.

At home, Robbie ate dinner in stony silence. And that night, his homework lay untouched on his bedroom desk. The next day at school, he went through his classes as if he had blinders on. Everything he did was in slow motion. And he was the last one to arrive for team practice, walking, not running, onto the field forty-five minutes late.

Coach Franklin called him over to the sidelines. "Why are you late, Robbie?"

"I got hung up. Sorry."

"That's not a good excuse!"

"It's the only one I have."

"Robbie, listen, you have a decision to make. I want you to go home now and think about it. You can't come late to practice without a good excuse. This is a baseball *team*. You have a responsibility to your teammates. They have to be able to rely on you.

"What this team needs now is a good catcher. Mojo's finger hasn't healed enough for him to catch. That's why I'm playing him at first. The second-string catcher from last year, Tug Peters, is okay. But I think you could be better. Of all the positions, you play catcher the best. The only other competition is Mosely."

"Eddie Mosely?"

"Hello? Is anybody home in there?" said the coach, pointing to Robbie's forehead. "Yes, Mosely. That's who I said. So you have to decide whether you're going to play where you can do your best and help the team the most. Or whether you're going to play at all. Don't come back tomorrow unless you're ready to do your best. I want a whole new attitude from you, Robbie, a *team* attitude. Or else I don't want to see you on this field again. I'll see you tomorrow, I hope." Coach Franklin turned around and resumed practice.

As Robbie walked away, he thought he caught resentful glances from more players than just Mosely. Not long afterward, he ran into Melinda and Brian.

"Say, don't you have practice now?" asked Melinda.

"Yeah, Robbie, why aren't you at practice?" piped up Brian.

"Coach told me to go home early."

"Early? That doesn't sound like the Coach Franklin I know. C'mon, Robbie, what—"

"Look, I got to go now," Robbie said, cutting off his friend.

Robbie began hurrying away when Melinda

called after him. "Hey, what about the tutoring we scheduled for tonight?"

Robbie shouted back over his shoulder. "Um, not tonight, Melinda. Maybe tomorrow. See you." Before he turned around again, Robbie saw the puzzled looks on his friends' faces.

He kept jogging. *Feels good to run, actually. Kind of get to like it after you get used to it.* He passed by the outdoor track and saw Ralph Butler doing some fast-paced work. Robbie turned into the track and caught up with Ralph.

"Well, well, well, if it isn't the baseball slowpoke!" said Ralph, grinning wide as he chugged along. It was an effort for Robbie to keep pace. *I have been loafing during conditioning,* he thought.

"I don't know about baseball anymore, Ralph. Maybe I'll take up track, give you a little competition."

Ralph stopped so suddenly that Robbie nearly tripped, trying to stop with him. "How come you don't sound like you're kidding?" Ralph asked.

"Coach Franklin wants me to be a catcher. I was born to be a pitcher."

"That's the coach's call, Robbie. You know that."

"The coach can be wrong, despite his famous two rules."

"So can we all, man. Even volcanoes like you. Let's get running some more. Things always seem clearer to me when I run."

Ralph sped off around the track again. Robbie

followed. The pace was furious, which suited Robbie fine this afternoon.

As they ran, they talked. Ralph talked more, since Robbie kept running out of breath. Ever since Ralph was a kid, he told Robbie, baseball had always looked great to him. But he never played much. That's because he'd been winning track events ever since he took the Charleston Peewee Marathon when he was seven. He found he loved running, and he wanted to spend all his time doing it.

Still, he had a yearning to play baseball. That's when he decided to try out for the team. But very quickly he discovered how hard it was to pick up. It would take him years to get even the basics down! Besides, baseball would take time away from track. And without the track scholarship he hoped for, college would remain a dream.

Gasping now, Robbie asked for a rest. As he caught his breath, he told Ralph his main goal was to be a major-league player. He'd also like to get a college education. Ralph gave him a thumbs-up handshake and said, "Hear that? You want to be a major-league *player*, not necessarily a *pitcher*. I've got to get back to my workout, Robbie. I'll check you later." Waving goodbye, Ralph headed down the track again.

Robbie walked home, thinking all the way. He entered the front door and bounded upstairs. After taking a quick shower, he got dressed and went back downstairs. He watched some TV until his parents got home. His mother walked in first.

63

"Hi, Mom!"

"Hi, Robbie! Your father home yet?"

"Nope. How'd your day go?"

"Oh, the usual. Hectic. Any preference for dinner tonight?"

"Not beets. Anything else is fine."

Robbie's mother laughed. The two of them had a running joke about red beets, which she knew Robbie hated. Outside, a car pulled into the driveway. "I think that's your father."

Sure enough, Mr. Belmont walked in the door a few seconds later. He kissed his wife, then said, "Hi, Robbie!"

"Hi, Dad!"

Mr. Belmont looked more closely at his son. "You okay, Robbie? Seems something is bothering you. Wouldn't be a girl now, would it?" Mr. Belmont winked at his wife.

"Oh, no, nothing like that. It's, uh, baseball."

"I should have guessed," said Mr. Belmont, taking a seat in the living room. "What's the problem?"

Robbie told his father about his day at practice. St. Simon Belmont listened carefully to his son, though sports weren't really his passion. He taught English at nearby Fuller University. Robbie always thought of his dad as a quiet man, not at all athletic like his mom. Ellen Reed, which was her name before marrying St. Simon Belmont, had won two national swimming championships in college. And she still looked as if she could compete today.

"Hmm," said Mr. Belmont, scratching his chin. "You know, Robbie, I once knew a guy who wanted to be a rock-and-roll star. This guy played electric lead guitar in high school. He'd play the school dances with his band, and the girls went wild over him." Ellen Belmont cleared her throat and sat next to her husband. Mr. Belmont looked at her and continued.

"Um, the girls started to take an interest in him, anyway. Later, in college, the band had a strong local following. They drew bigger and bigger crowds to the halls they played in. Pretty soon, they were the hottest thing in town. Then, an agent caught their act at a club. He lined up a gig for them, an important gig, too—opening for the Rolling Stones at the Helix. This was an arena that held 19,000 people. All the big rock acts played there. But the agent had one condition."

Mr. Belmont paused, remembering. His face clouded for a moment. Ellen Belmont reached over and touched his hand.

"The agent said they could do the gig if they replaced their lead electric guitarist with someone else, someone the agent had in mind. The band refused. But their lead guitarist told them it was the break of a lifetime, to take it without him. So they did the gig with another lead guitarist. And they changed the name of the band from St. Simon and the Salty Dogs to just the Salty Dogs."

"What?" blurted Robbie, jumping up in excitement. "You were once with the Salty Dogs?

As lead guitarist? WOW! I hear that band played all the time on classic rock stations. They were great! I mean, really great!"

Suddenly, Robbie realized his father had played with them *before* they ever recorded. "Gosh, Dad, that must be rough. You know, just missing out on something like that."

"For a while, Robbie, it *was* rough. But I got over it. The agent was right. The guitarist who replaced me was ten times better than I was. And he made the difference in the band. They went on to fame, and I went on to become a college English teacher.

"The point is, Robbie, you don't want to go down the baseball trail halfway as a pitcher, then find out you don't have what it takes to make the big leagues. I was a good guitarist, but not good enough for the 'big leagues,' the big arenas and stadiums. Go with what you do best, Robbie. That's what I think Coach Franklin is trying to get you to do. I'm happy I stayed in college and got my degrees. That's where I met your mother, you know." Ellen Belmont smiled and squeezed her husband's hand.

Despite his father's efforts to lift his spirits, Robbie climbed the stairs to his room at a speed of about ten yards an hour. He'd made up his mind that afternoon. *If the coach is not interested in my pitching, I am not interested in playing for the coach.*

Robbie picked up the Eddie Trent ball by his bedside and tossed it up a few times. Suddenly,

66

he saw himself throwing it right through the glass of his bedroom window. But before he could actually do it, the phone rang. It was Brian Webster.

"Robbie, I just read an interview with Eddie Trent about catching! He said a minor-league coach once told him the quickest way to the majors is to be either a pitcher or a catcher! That's when Trent concentrated on being a catcher!"

"You're kidding!"

"Honest."

There was a silence while Robbie took in Brian's words. Snapping to again, Robbie told Brian he was sorry he hadn't made the team.

"I want to come to practices, though," Brian said. "I just want to be around the game. And I really like Coach Franklin, even though he was stupid to cut me. And by the way, Melinda is mad at you."

"Why?"

"I think you know why. Listen, I just wanted to tell you that bit about what Eddie Trent said. I got to go."

"Thanks, Brian."

"It's all right. Be cool."

"You, too."

Robbie hung up and looked at the ball in his hand. He was so used to fiddling with it that he hardly ever read what Eddie Trent had written on it. But now it seemed to jump out at him: "Great catch, kid! You came to play."

Chapter Nine

Next practice, Robbie came to play. His enthusiasm had returned. But he was unsure about shouting encouragements to the same players he had ignored for a week. Still, he began to work in a "Nice throw, Jonesy!" or "Good work, José!" when others would be saying similar things. Once, catching infield practice, he praised Mojo at first for a fine short-hop pickup. On hearing this, Coach Franklin raised his eyebrows.

But Robbie could tell most of the players were keeping their distance from him. It surprised him how hard this was to take. It stung. He was on the outside looking in. Robbie now knew he had to prove himself not only as a catcher, but also as a person who could be trusted.

Eddie Mosely had been taunting him steadily since he arrived early for practice. Mosely was the master of the unoriginal remark. His first one to Robbie was no exception. "Well lookee here, fellas! If it isn't Big Boy, coming to practice *on time* for a change! We should all bow down in thanks!" More than a few players laughed when Mosely said this. What really hurt Robbie was that there was truth in it.

After some batting and infield practice, Coach Franklin organized a game, putting the current best bets for starters on one team. Robbie's jaw fell when he saw that Eddie Mosely was starting at catcher! A fire flared up in his stomach. Robbie felt his lungs squeeze closed.

Then, for the second team, Coach Franklin named last year's second-string catcher, Tug Peters. He was a big, likable guy who was almost but not quite fat. Robbie couldn't believe it. *You mean I'm not even going to play?* But the coach came over, slapped him on the back, and said, "Robbie, you'll come in after Eddie and Tug are through. Meanwhile, I want you to warm up a few of these pitchers you see around here. They look cold, don't they?" He said it loud enough for the pitchers to hear. Coach Franklin wanted to break the ice as much as Robbie did.

So Robbie warmed up pitchers while the game began without him. He didn't consider what he was doing an especially exciting task. But he did it with as much hustle as he could muster. In the second inning, when the starters were at bat, Mojo wandered over and watched. After a few pitches, he began commenting on how Robbie was catching the ball. Robbie hadn't given much attention to the details of "catching the ball." *It's thrown to me and I catch it. What's the big deal?*

First, Mojo moved Robbie up much closer to

69

the plate than he had been. Robbie could hardly believe that he could be so close to the plate and not interfere with the batter's swing. But Mojo told him it was the right distance because the batter steps *away* from the catcher. Robbie's ears burned when Mojo pointed to Mosely and said, "See where he's playing? Mosely's been catching all through grade school. You can learn a lot from watching him. See how close to the batter his glove is? You want to be as close as possible because it makes the throw to second base quicker. Also, where your glove is when you catch the ball may influence how the umpire calls the pitch. If a curve comes over the plate in the strike zone and you catch it way back there, it looks more like a ball to the ump."

The pitcher whom Robbie was warming up was also a freshman. He was about six feet four inches tall but very skinny. He had a whippy, jumping fast ball, and his arm never seemed to throw from the same angle twice in a row. His name was Bill Wirick, and everyone called him Wire.

He threw a sidearm fast ball that bent outward, just ticking the outside corner. When Robbie caught it, Mojo suddenly yelled, "Freeze that glove! Look where it is! It's a foot out of the strike zone!" It was true. Robbie had caught the pitch and let its natural momentum carry his glove a little.

"You have to *frame* that pitch for the umpire, Robbie," continued Mojo. "Keep the glove in the

70

strike zone whenever you can. Even if the pitch is outside it, you may still get a close call to go your way. If your glove is in the strike zone, an ump may think that's where the ball came in. Use your webbing to catch pitches just outside. Remember, you have to frame those suckers!" Mojo turned and left. He was on deck to bat.

So Robbie got into framing each pitch he caught. The warm-ups became a challenge as he began mastering this skill, learning its smallest details. Wire, finished with his warm-ups, thanked Robbie for the nice target he made with his glove. Robbie was surprised at how much better this made him feel.

Finally, it was Robbie's turn to catch in the practice game. He trudged over to where the catcher's gear had been piled. It looked as if someone had kicked the equipment into a jumble. *Funny,* thought Robbie, *Tug's usually a lot neater than this.* As Robbie reached down for the top piece, a voice shouted out from the bench. "Don't stink it up, Big Boy!" Robbie looked over and saw Mosely sitting there with a wide grin on his face.

First, Robbie put on the shin guards. They protected the lower leg from nasty foul tips, dirt-eating pitches, and flashing spikes sliding home. Each shin guard was in three hard-plastic sections hinged together with canvas. One section covered the knee. Another, the long middle slab, shielded the shin. And a flappy lower part covered the instep of the foot. Robbie buckled

71

them on. But where was the chest protector?

"Yo, Big Boy! Missing something?" Eddie Mosely was laughing as he dangled the chest protector by a strap and jiggled it.

Robbie was steamed. He walked toward the bench to get the chest protector from Mosely. But as he walked, a buckle on each shin guard came loose. He rebuckled, walked some more, and two others came undone. He bent over to examine the problem, and Mosely's voice rang out again. "Been catching long, Belmont?" Some snorts of laughter came from other players on the bench. Mosely wasn't through, either. "When you put shin guards on the wrong legs, Big Boy, the buckles rub against each other. That's why they pop open when you walk. Quick quiz—do you know what hand the catcher's mitt is supposed to go on? Or should I stick around and show you?"

Robbie took off the shin guards and put them on correctly. He said nothing and looked at no one. Then he went over and yanked the chest protector from Mosely's hand. Robbie knew Mosely and some of his chums were now watching to see if he knew how to wear it. The large, dark blue, ribbed pad had a twisted strap arrangement. *It looks like Mosely twisted it some more before giving it to me!* But Robbie managed to smooth it out. He put his arms in the right spots and buckled the chest protector up firmly. It smelled damp and dusty, but Robbie felt good in it.

He hustled to the catcher's box to catch the warm-up pitches from Wire. This was Wire's first time pitching in high school. Robbie understood what he was going through.

Coach Franklin, who was umpiring, called "Batter up!" This was Robbie's cue to take the last warm-up pitch and peg it to second base. But in his eagerness to throw the fastest peg he could, Robbie hurled it over the second baseman's head. The ball skipped into center field. Mosely and his friends let loose some moose calls from the bench. Robbie's face turned as red as a tomato.

"All right, all right," said the coach. "The first time at anything is rough. Let's whip that ball around the infield."

The ball was retrieved, tossed around the infield, and finally returned to Wire. Robbie joined him on the mound to discuss signals. One finger down was a fast ball. Two fingers down meant a curve.

"And what do you throw when I have three fingers down, Wire?"

"Well, a split-fingered fast ball, I guess."

"Right," said Robbie. He had seen Wire's split-fingered fast ball a few times during warm-ups. Wire couldn't control it very well, but it sank viciously. "And four's a change-up."

"What about a pitchout?" asked Wire.

"Oh, right." *Forgot about that!*

"A catcher I used to play with used a closed fist," said Wire.

"Closed fist it is. Okay, let's get 'em."

Robbie trotted back to his new position, and Coach Franklin handed him his last piece of catcher's equipment. It was all black. There was black leather-covered cushioning on the inside. There were black metal bars to peer through. *Like my face is in jail!* A black throat protector dangled down. *Makes me look a little like a turkey!* And black canvas straps held the whole two pounds of it on his head. It was the guardian of the catcher's face. It was the iron mask.

Eagle Wilson was the first batter. *A weak hitter, grounds out,* remembered Robbie. Although he didn't know it, he was starting to build a mental catalogue of hitters.

Oh, right! Robbie thought. *I have to call the pitch!* He remembered how important it was for the pitcher to get a strike on the first pitch. Brian had told him that four of five walks began with the count at one ball, no strikes. He also said that twice as many runs resulted from a 1–0 count than a count of 0–1. A fast ball was easiest to control. So Robbie put down one finger.

"Here comes the fast ball, Eagle!" Mosely's voice called out. *I didn't hide my sign!* Robbie thought with alarm. Wire slung his long thin arm straight down overhead, and the ball lined in, rising a bit at the end. Eagle didn't swing. Robbie caught the ball and pulled his glove down slightly, into the top of the strike zone. But the coach called "Ball one!"

Robbie turned around without thinking and said, "Ball? That was—"

He never finished. Coach Franklin whipped off his own mask dramatically and made a grand gesture to the sidelines. "Yer out of the game!" he shouted. The coach then turned quickly around and started kicking dirt onto Robbie's shin guards. Robbie stood there, stunned.

The rest of the team got a big kick out of this. They were still laughing as Coach Franklin said quietly to Robbie, "That's the last time you will ever turn around to an umpire and complain. It's the worst thing you can do. It makes the close calls go against you. A catcher must always be polite with the umpire, especially if it's his coach! Never turn around to question a call. Ask him about the pitch a few pitches later. And be honest. You know as well as I do that fast ball rose high, and you jerked the mitt too far. But good try at framing, not bad for a rookie! Play ball!"

One ball, no strikes. *Last pitch was too high? Eagle hits grounders. Pitch him low! Curve or sinker to go low? Or low fast ball? Low fast ball. We need a strike here.* So Robbie started to give the fast ball signal, but remembered he had to disguise it. He didn't want Mosely razzing him again. Coach Franklin leaned forward and whispered, "Use your glove hanging off your left knee to hide your signal."

Robbie did just that, giving the signal for a fast ball. He set up a knee-high target, lowest line of the strike zone. Then it occurred to him that Eagle wasn't *that* good of a hitter, so he raised the target slightly. This time, Wire threw it in with a sidearm swipe, and it went right to Robbie's glove.

"Strike!" the coach called. Then, in a softer voice, he asked, "Why did you hold a lower target that time, Robbie?"

Robbie didn't want Eagle to hear his answer, so he whispered to the coach. "Because Eagle tends to hit grounders."

"Very smart!" Coach Franklin whispered back, grinning and enjoying himself.

One ball, one strike. Let's try the curve. He seemed to have pretty good control of it, thought Robbie. *And he controlled his overhead curve better than his three-quarter, sidearm, or underhand-sweep curve.* But Robbie had no signal for what arm motion Wire should use. Robbie called "Time" and jogged out to Wire.

"Wire, did you know you have better control of your overhead curve than any other curve?"

"I do?"

"Seems like it."

"So you're going to call a curve, but you want it to be a strike. Overhead curve, huh?"

"Exactly."

"Okay, you got it, Robbie," Wire said.

The overhead curve, sure enough, dipped down nicely across the low outside strike zone. Eagle swung and missed. But Robbie blinked, shutting his glove a split second too soon. The ball nicked the edge of his mitt and bounced wildly past the backstop. *Passed ball!*

Robbie whipped off his mask and chased down the ball. He picked it up and rifled it back to Wire on the mound. Then Robbie hurried back to home plate and put on his mask again.

"Good eye, Big Boy!" whooped Mosely from the bench.

Robbie clenched his teeth. *Will this guy ever let up?* Then he muttered to the coach, "I always blink when the batter swings."

"Keep your mouth open," Coach Franklin said. "It's unnatural to blink if your mouth's open. Try it."

Robbie kept his mouth open on the next pitch. Eagle swung and dribbled a foul ball outside the first-base line. Robbie didn't blink! "Thanks, Coach. It works."

One ball, two strikes. Let Wire throw that wild, sinking, split-fingered fast ball, out of the strike zone even! Make Eagle fish for it. Robbie started to enjoy choosing the pitches. He was trying to outguess the guesses of the batter. It was a game within the game. He snapped down three fingers and gave a low, outside target.

Wire threw it sidearm, and Eagle lunged for it. The bat chopped down and ticked the tiniest bit of the ball's underbelly. Just a tiny, tiny thing, but suddenly a big *BONG* rocked Robbie's head back. The ticked ball had angled up and crashed into Robbie's iron mask.

Robbie had seen this happen many times on TV and in games he'd played. Like everyone else, when a foul tip hit the catcher in the mask, he'd think, *Good thing he was wearing a mask. Let's get on with the game.* But this was the first time Robbie had ever experienced it personally. What they didn't tell you was that it jarred your head completely out of thought for a few seconds. The ringing in your ears lasted just as long.

When Robbie came out of it, he couldn't believe Mosely was cackling at him again. "Hey, Big Boy, answer that phone ringing in your ears!"

The coach called out, "Have some respect, Mosely!" Mosely stopped laughing.

Coach Franklin then turned to Robbie. "Son, you've just had your bell rung. In the name of Roy Campanella, Yogi Berra, Carlton Fisk, Mickey Cochrane, Johnny Bench, Gary Carter, and Eddie Trent, welcome to the catching club! All those who've been bonged in the mask salute you! You've only been catcher for five pitches so far, and a lot has happened, no? Interesting position, don't you think?"

Chapter Ten

After practice, Robbie felt like a damp dish-rag. His shirt was soaked with sweat. All the squatting he had done left his knees and leg muscles sore. The passed ball he had chased down at least made him run. *Gave me a chance to stretch my legs! You can go stir crazy back there!*

Coach Franklin had asked him to stay behind for a bit after practice. While the coach spoke with Mojo and a few other players, Robbie helped the coach's student assistant gather the equipment. His name was Joshua Kenny. He knew baseball inside and out, even though he couldn't play it the way other boys could. Joshua had been born unable to straighten his legs. He got around, as he described it, "by swiveling like someone permanently doing the Twist."

Joshua complimented Robbie on his catching. He also said he was glad to see Robbie back on the team. "You're an incredible hitter," he said, reaching down for a bat.

After they had packed away almost all the

equipment, Joshua asked Robbie to pitch him a few. "I want to try out a new batting stance," he said with a little smile.

"Sure," said Robbie. "Always glad to pitch a few."

So he lobbed Josh a few. Joshua's scrunched stance *was* unusual, but rather ingenious in its own way. Since he couldn't step into the pitch, he relied on his powerful arms to hit. Several clean, sharp singles whizzed over Robbie's head. Robbie felt surprisingly proud each time Josh connected. He swung and missed about half the time.

"Way to go, slugger!" Robbie called. Then Joshua headed out to fetch the balls from the outfield. "Let me get them, Joshua."

"I can get them! You've been working your tail off!"

"How about if I get the ones on this side?"

"Okay."

By the time they had retrieved everything, Coach Franklin was alone and waiting on the bench. "Nice hitting there, Josh!" he called. Joshua smiled and went about the business of rounding up towels and the water bucket.

The coach turned to Robbie. "You did real well out there today. I just wanted to tell you that I'm pleased with the improvement in your attitude. I think you and catching go well together."

"I never knew how much a catcher did!" Robbie felt as if he had learned a thousand things about catching in just this first day, and had a billion more to go.

"Mosely and Tug are still catching better than you. But you have an excellent chance to beat them out. It depends on how naturally you take to the position, and how well you learn. So be sure to keep up your schoolwork. Catching is physically demanding, but it's also the most thinking position."

Joshua chugged by with an armload of towels. He was barely able to carry them and the water bucket together. "Coach," he said, "I know I'm your assistant, but what about an assistant's assistant?"

"What about Brian Webster?" blurted Robbie. "He'd love to help out, Coach. And he knows as much about baseball as Josh here. Brian would be great!" *And I could use another friendly face around here myself*, thought Robbie. Eddie Mosely had definitely gotten under his skin.

"Hmm," said the coach. "You may be right, Robbie. I'll give Brian a call as soon as I get home. What's his number?" He took out a notebook and wrote down the phone number Robbie gave him.

"Tell me about Wire on the mound today," Coach Franklin went on. "Sometimes, he looks unhittable. Other times, he looks like a batters' picnic."

"He's wild. That's his main problem," Robbie said. "And when he gets behind in the count, he starts aiming the ball rather than throwing it naturally."

"That's when his pitches start to lose speed and movement," added the coach.

"Yeah, they lose something, all right. The guy loves to throw all out. I can tell. And he hates it when he pitches too carefully. He has all these different throwing angles just begging to be used!"

The thought of the tall Wirick pitching from these angles brought a smile to the coach's face. "You know, Robbie, I see Wire thirty pounds heavier down the road. And I like what I see. Can you imagine him tall and strong instead of tall and skinny? *With* control? If you can help him get his pitches more under control while still throwing free, we'll have a real winner on our hands!"

Coach Franklin and Robbie talked a bit more about the other pitchers. Then the coach drove Robbie and Joshua home. Robbie felt a tiny but special glow inside him. He was entering the coach's world so directly. He also enjoyed goofing around with Joshua, who was fast becoming a friend.

Robbie was still in a good mood after dinner. That's when he gave Melinda a call. "Hello? Melinda? It's Robbie. Um, Brian said you were mad at me or something."

"I? Mad at the great Robbie Belmont? How could that *possibly* be?" Her voice dripped with acid. "I *enjoy* sacrificing my free time so that some bigheaded jock can squeeze by in his schoolwork to stay on the team. And I *love* being stood up. Why would I be mad?"

"Look, I'm really sorry about all that," said

83

Robbie. "I know I haven't been very friendly lately. But you know how much baseball means to me. I . . . I apologize."

"That didn't hurt now, did it?" Melinda was still angry.

"I know I should have called a while ago. But I had some things to straighten out. Now they're straightened out." Robbie paused, then continued. "Could we pick up where we left off? I still need a tutor, and you're the best one I could have."

"The *only* one," Melinda said. "No one else is crazy enough to try to help you study." She let out a long breath over the phone. "Okay, okay, I forgive you. Give me five minutes, and I'll be over. BE THERE THIS TIME! I intend to put you through a little math torture. It'll serve you right!"

"Thanks, Melinda."

"You're welcome. Soon, goon."

" 'Bye."

Melinda was in the middle of trying to get Robbie to understand some basics of statistics and probability theory when Brian came over.

"Robbie! Coach just asked me to be one of his assistants! I'm a happy young man again! He said it was your suggestion. Thanks."

"Your being there is going to help me a lot, Brian. That Mosely guy is really getting on my nerves."

"Oh, hi, Melinda," said Brian. "Still trying to pound some sense into Robbie, I see."

"It's a dirty job, but somebody has to do it," she said with a laugh.

"Are *you* mad at me, Brian?" asked Robbie.

"Me? Melinda's the one who's mad at you!"

"She says you are."

"We both are!" they said together, then cracked up. Robbie sat there sheepishly.

"Don't look so solemn, Robbie," Melinda said, smiling. "You're back in our good graces again. We'll still speak with you from time to time. Now let's finish this chapter on statistics and maybe we'll let you buy us some pizza."

"I brought my history book," said Brian. "I can study while you finish."

"Why do I have to know statistics?" Robbie asked, groaning. "I'll never need it in real life!"

"Are you crazy?" said Brian, his eyes bugging out, the history book in his hand already forgotten. "A catcher's always using statistics! I can show you. What problem are you working on?"

Melinda showed Brian the problem. After a moment of thinking, Brian translated the dry math into a language Robbie could understand—baseball. "Let's see, 'Event A happens thirty percent of the time; event B, fifty percent. If A happens, B will happen ninety percent of the time.' That's like, say, Eagle gets his first pitch over for a strike thirty percent of the time. That would be event A. And event B could mean his average percent for getting his second pitch over: fifty percent of the time. But if he gets his first pitch over, event A, that means event B, his rate of getting the second pitch over, goes up to ninety percent!"

This time, it was Melinda who looked lost and Robbie who understood immediately. But it didn't take long for Melinda to figure out how to get Robbie to understand math. Use baseball for examples!

All three finished their homework and walked to the pizza parlor. Robbie asked Melinda if she would be interested in making statistic charts on the team pitchers and the opponents' batters. She didn't like the idea at all and mentioned all the other activities she had.

At the pizza parlor, they found Joshua Kenny sitting at a table. He was munching on a pepperoni slice while reading *The Call of the Wild* for English class. Joshua waved, and they went over. He was glad to meet Brian and find out he was the new assistant. Melinda already knew Josh from English class. The two quickly fell into a discussion about the book Josh was reading. Robbie and Brian went to the counter and ordered.

"There's something different about Melinda when she talks about English instead of math," Robbie said to Brian. Both boys peered back at the table. Melinda was leaning toward Joshua as they discussed the book.

"Either that," said Brian with a little smile, "or there's something different about her when she talks with Joshua instead of you."

They sneaked another peek back at the table.

Melinda and Joshua both suddenly erupted into laughter at something.

"But what do I know?" said Brian, shrugging his shoulders.

They got the pizza and went back to the table. It seemed Melinda and Joshua had barely noticed they were gone.

The pizza parlor was right next to the library. As Robbie, Melinda, Joshua, and Brian were finishing eating, a bunch of baseball players came in. Eagle Wilson was among them. They all greeted Joshua right away. Then they said hello to Robbie, Brian, and Melinda. Cynthia Wu was with Eagle, and she said hello, too.

Eagle complimented Robbie for hitting a double off him during the inter-squad game. "I should have thrown you a curve instead of the inside fast ball Mosely called for," he said.

"That's convenient!" Cynthia remarked. "A pitcher can blame the catcher's signals when the batter gets a hit, then claim the credit when the batter gets out!"

Robbie thought Cynthia's comment had some truth to it, although Eagle seemed to feel it was a bit unfair. Before Robbie and his friends left, he chatted briefly with Cynthia. She asked how practice was going, and Robbie told her. He even grew comfortable enough with her to mention his problems with Mosely.

Cynthia said she understood. Then she told Robbie that Eagle had complained about what a sloppy target Mosely offered when catching.

"You'll beat him out! I have a strong feeling about that!" she said.

Something about the way she said it made Robbie believe it. *She has a real nice voice,* he thought, *low and warm. Am I starting to like her? Not too fast there, guy! She happens to be the girlfriend of the starting pitcher. It wouldn't be too smart to fall for her in that way.*

So far, Robbie had never "fallen" for anyone. He remembered back to what his dad said before their long talk together. "Seems something is bothering you. Wouldn't be a girl now, would it?" It wasn't then. But Robbie wasn't sure now. He knew he liked the look in Cynthia's eyes when she said, "I'm glad to see you and Brian getting along so well." *That's right!* Robbie thought. *She saw us angry at each other that one day by the elm outside the parking lot!*

Robbie, Brian, and Melinda walked Joshua home. Melinda and Josh were pretty funny, making up "dog dialogue" for *The Call of the Wild.* But Robbie kept thinking of that look in Cynthia's eyes. *Enough of this,* he told himself. *This romance stuff is too distracting. And I don't see what good can come of it at this stage of my baseball career.*

The three friends said goodbye to Joshua in front of his house and walked on. Halfway down the street, Melinda turned to look once more at where Josh lived. Then she said, "You know, maybe I could work on some stat sheets for your baseball team after all, Robbie. I can hang out at a few practices, take a few notes. It may even help me help you in your math."

"Great, Melinda!" Robbie thought, *And that means you'd also be spending some more time around Joshua.* But he didn't think he should say that out loud. He didn't know enough about this romance stuff yet to trust his opinions.

Chapter Eleven

More than ever, Robbie wanted to win the starting catching spot in the season opener, which was fast approaching. His strong hitting and growing knowledge of catching moved him from third to second string. Tug Peters, the guy Robbie passed, took the news well. But Mosely, for all of his sourness, continued to perform like an old hand behind the plate. Robbie had mixed feelings about that. For the sake of the team, he wanted Mosely to do his best. But Robbie couldn't help smiling inwardly when the loudmouth flubbed a short hopper or struck out.

Having Brian Webster around was always helpful. Most of the guys liked Brian, and that helped ease Robbie into the company of his teammates. Mosely started making his remarks and practical jokes less public. But they were still just as irritating. Hiding the catcher's mask was one stunt he pulled. *Ha-ha*, thought Robbie. *Great humor, Moze.* Another Mosely trick was talking nonstop while Robbie was batting and he was catching. *Made a lot worse by the fact that he was boring!*

Brian urged Robbie to dish it back at Mosely.

"You've been taking it quietly long enough. Time to turn the tables!"

The next time Robbie was batting, Mosely started jabbering about the weather and the color of the dirt and other exciting topics. Robbie stepped out of the batter's box. Then he turned around and asked Mosely in a louder-than-usual voice, "Do you want to talk or play ball?"

Mosely was clearly surprised by this outburst. Robbie pressed on. "Which is it, talk or play?"

Coach Franklin was again umpiring. He felt it gave him a good view of his players. The coach said nothing, waiting with Robbie for Mosely's response.

Finally, Mosely said, "What do you want to do, Big Boy, play or whine?"

"I'll wait, Mosely."

"Coach, how long is a batter allowed to stay out of the batter's box?"

"If he's involved in some dispute with an opposing player, a batter's time limit is suspended," the coach said. Then he added, "So maybe you should shut up and catch, Mosely. I'm getting tired of hearing your gums flap today. Batter up!"

Robbie took a few deep breaths and stepped back into the batter's box. Mosely was silent, but Robbie could almost hear him fuming. Eagle Wilson looked in for the signal from Mosely, but shook it off. This was about the tenth time Robbie had faced Eagle since practices began. He was getting to know Eagle's pitching style better and better. He had never caught for Eagle in a real scrimmage yet, but he had warmed him up before.

Eagle finally accepted a sign from Mosely after shaking off three. *He's a bit choosy in pitch selection!* Robbie thought. Eagle went into his wind-up, a classic-looking wind-up, every part perfect. *Almost too perfect*, Robbie thought. *Eagle didn't throw the ball in—he smoothed it in.*

The pitch came into the low outside strike zone. It was a tough pitch to hit, but Robbie was ready. He swung with pure joy, barely feeling a thing in his bat as he swatted the ball. There was just a sweet crunch.

The whole team stopped to watch the ball sail deeper and deeper. It was a powerful shot, a clean homer. Robbie trotted around the bases, tilting his head slightly down. He was thinking, *Humble! Keep it humble!* while nearly bursting with satisfaction.

"Hey, Belmont, you beat my distance record!" José Sanchez shouted good-naturedly from center field. "But not for lo-ong!"

Other moments were not so happy for Robbie. One occurred the first time he tried to throw out a runner stealing second with a left-hander batting. His throw went two inches and whammed into the left-hander's bat. The ball ricocheted from the bat to the unprotected side of Robbie's neck. *Whap!* The runner went to third as Robbie looked around in a daze for the ball. He couldn't see it anywhere. Finally, Wire raced in from the mound and picked the ball up—right next to Robbie's foot!

Together, Melinda, Brian, and Robbie created a useful stat sheet for the team pitchers. Melinda filled it out the few times a week she came to practice. Robbie noticed that when Melinda was around, Joshua seemed *especially* interested in those stat sheets.

Filled in, the stat sheet showed ball-and-strike counts, what pitches were thrown, and where. Melinda then put the stat sheet information into a computer program she had devised on her home computer. It took a while to build up enough statistics for reliable patterns to emerge. But finally one day she had some interesting news for Robbie.

"About forty percent of Eagle's strikes are on the outside corner, and forty percent are through the heart of the strike zone. Only about twenty percent are on the inside corner. But when he does hit the inside corner, the batter does nothing with it about ninety percent of the time!"

"Then he doesn't work the inside corner half enough!"

"You could say that," said Melinda, smiling.

"That makes his outside strikes easier to hit because they're easier to predict!" chimed in Brian.

"Right!" Melinda exclaimed, rustling through about ten sheets of computer printout. "Here it is. Outside corner effectiveness, Eagle Wilson: twenty-nine percent. It's obvious batters are waiting on his outside pitch. And when they get it, *whack*!"

Despite his competition with Mosely, Robbie knew he shouldn't keep this information to himself. The next practice, he reported it to Coach Franklin. The coach was very surprised and obviously pleased. Seeing Melinda in the bleachers, he went over and thanked her. Coach Franklin shared the information with Mosely and Eagle privately. Neither of them, however, seemed to use it much in the last inter-squad game before the season opener.

Robbie was sitting on the bench as the starters played. In the middle of the third inning, Melinda waved him over to the bleachers. "Same old pattern for Eagle," she said, looking toward the mound. "He's even more off than usual—just seventeen percent inside strikes."

"Hmm," said Robbie softly. "Thanks for the information, Melinda. I better get back now."

Not long after Robbie took his seat on the bench, Coach Franklin walked over to him. "Go in for Mosely after this inning, Robbie. I want to see what you can do with the starters."

When the third inning was over, Robbie walked over to the heap of catcher's equipment Mosely had just taken off. The mask wasn't in the pile. Robbie was fed up. He called out to Mosely, "You had the mask last, Mosely. It's not here where it should be. Find it and bring it to me. I have to go warm up Eagle." Robbie stalked to the catcher's box.

Mosely didn't have any choice and he knew it. He trotted out with the mask after Robbie had pegged a right-on-the-bag throw to second base. "Thanks, Eddie," Robbie said, taking the black iron face protector from him.

"You'll blow it, Big Boy," said Mosely, turning to go back to the bench. Robbie went out to get his signals straight with Eagle. For Eagle, one finger down was an across-the-seams fast ball that tended to rise—a "lifter." Two fingers down meant a fast ball gripped with the seams. It tended to sail out—a "sailer." Three fingers down meant a fast ball thrown with extra pressure on the middle finger. This pitch cut in to a right-handed batter—a "cutter." Four fingers down signaled a curve, and five fingers down meant a change-up.

Robbie told Eagle he was going to set up a lot of low, inside targets. Eagle told him it was hard for him to throw inside. "I once broke my little brother's ankle with a pitch. His foot was in a cast for six weeks."

"Oh," said Robbie. He didn't want to urge Eagle to do something against his will. Besides, Robbie hadn't even caught one pitch yet for the starters. It might be a bit uppity for him to start telling Eagle what to do.

On the other hand, Eagle could be a much better pitcher if he started throwing inside more. Brian had assured Robbie that every major-league pitcher favored working the batter inside-outside. Pitching inside first pushed the batter back a little, setting him up for an outside pitch. *I'll have to think about this*, thought Robbie.

He trotted back behind the plate, putting his mask on as he did. "Says he broke his brother's ankle once with an inside pitch," Robbie said quietly to the coach. "So now he's afraid to throw inside."

"He's going to have to work on that," the coach said.

As Eagle pitched, Robbie moved his mitt farther inside. It didn't stop Eagle's outside placement much, but at least it started getting him used to the idea. Robbie also started calling for a lot of cutter fast balls. These bent in to a right-hander and moved toward the inside corner more and more. Eagle seemed to find his cutter fast ball easier to get inside.

The curve was extra hard for Eagle to keep away from the outside corner. To get a curve to cross the inside corner, he had to start it out aimed directly at the batter. So Robbie kept putting down a lot of three-fingered signals for the cutter fast ball. There were so many that Eagle eventually got tired of shaking them off. *Maybe he's even starting to enjoy all the extra strikeouts he's getting!*

Between innings, Melinda told Robbie that Eagle hadn't thrown that many cutter fast balls before. However, when he got them over, they were seventy-five percent effective. The problem had been that he threw most of them for balls. But after a few innings of Robbie's frequent three-fingered signs, Eagle started to get more and more cutters across for strikes. *Practice helps!*

The game moved along rapidly. Eagle mowed down the majority of second-string batters with relative ease. Robbie put in a solid, workman-like catching performance. Nothing very unusual happened until the seventh inning.

Robbie was catching. The second-string team had men on second and third. There were no outs. The batter fouled off two bunt attempts. Then he tried a suicide squeeze. It was risky, since another bunt foul would mean a strikeout. The tough-to-bunt cutter fast ball rushed in. The batter squared around to make a do-or-die bunting try, and the ball just ticked the bat. Robbie hung in there, unblinking, and the ball went right into his glove. Then he stepped out in front of the plate and tagged the sliding runner who had tried to steal with the pitch.

The runner on second was caught midway between second and third. Where he'd run would depend on where Robbie threw the ball. Robbie realized that if he threw it to either base, the runner would easily make it to the other one.

As a pitcher, Robbie had often run into a similar situation. A base runner in a playful pickup game would take a *huge* lead midway down the base path. If the pitcher threw it to any base (stupidest choice: first base), the runner would make it easily to the other one. The way to stop this base-running ploy was to run like mad directly at the runner! Then, if he headed to either base, a quick toss would nail him.

So Robbie ran like crazy directly at the runner between second and third base. The runner, clearly startled, just stared at the catcher bolting toward him. By the time he made a motion toward third base, Robbie had tagged him.

Robbie was breathing heavily when he heard cheering and whooping going on around him. His teammates were charging him! *What did I do wrong? Why are they laughing at me?* he wondered. But then they were pounding him on his back and congratulating him, giving him high fives and low fives and middle twos. Brian yelled above the noise, "Robbie, you just made an unassisted triple play! An unassisted triple play!"

"What do you mean 'unassisted'?" said Robbie, smiling finally. "I couldn't have done it without you, Bri!"

The next day, Robbie had another reason to smile. Coach Franklin had posted the names of the players who had made the team on the locker-room bulletin board. They were listed in order. The first name given at each position was the starter. Under CATCHERS, Robbie read his name first. Eddie Mosely's name came next.

When Robbie turned away from the bulletin board, Mosely was standing right behind him. "We'll see, Big Boy. We'll see. Coach has been known to correct mistakes early. And *you* are a mistake as a starter."

Mosely stalked out of the locker room, leaving Robbie standing there like a statue.

Chapter Twelve

The opening game of the season was at home against the Fulton Bucks. Last year, they had eliminated the Riverton Tigers for the league championship. They started the same pitcher who had beaten the Tigers: Charles "Chainsaw" McKenzer. He was a big, strong, flat-topped, grunting monster of a pitcher whose fast ball, according to Mojo Johnson, made a buzzing sound when it went by.

"He looks like he's chewing tobacco," Robbie said to Mojo.

"He's not chewing tobacco, Robbie. He's gnawing on the side of his mouth."

"Looks like a mean dude, all right."

"He *is* a mean dude. I hear he even keeps his Walkman tuned to the easy listening station all day."

"Brrr! That could make you real mean."

"His curve is adequate," Mojo went on, "and he doesn't like to use a change-up because he thinks it's wimpy. Basically, everything he does is calculated to make you too terrified to swing."

Mojo gave Robbie a scouting report on the Bucks' starting lineup. He also established signs to flash Robbie about pitch selection from first base, the position Mojo now played. "I'll flash them *only* if you want them," he said.

Robbie felt eager and fresh, wearing his Tigers uniform for the first time, proud of the big number "8" on his back. It was a good catcher's number, the same as Yogi Berra's and Gary Carter's.

Mosely just glared at Robbie. A silent, surly presence on the bench, he followed Robbie's every move. Mojo noticed. So did Coach Franklin. He called Mosely over for a private talk. It was short and to the point. Then the coach sent Mosely back to the bench. The glares were gone. Mosely just sat there, usually looking at the ground. Robbie had a feeling this wouldn't be the end of his problems with Mosely.

Robbie glanced up at the bleachers and saw his parents sitting there with Riverton Tigers pennants in their hands. They smiled and waved at him. Sitting in front of them and right behind the bench was Melinda. She had the familiar stat sheet in her lap and was marking something down on it. Joshua sat next to her. As usual, he was talking.

But what surprised Robbie was seeing Cynthia Wu on the other side of Melinda. *Ah, she probably wanted to check out Melinda's stat sheet. Just to keep up on how Eagle is pitching. Figures.*

During batting practice, Robbie noticed in the

distance a tall figure in a red sweat suit jogging toward the playing field. *Ralph!* Robbie waved to him when he jogged into range. Ralph waved back. When he arrived at the bleachers, Ralph took a seat at the end.

The stands were not only packed, but also overflowing. No Riverton Tigers' fan could ever forget last year's extra-inning 3–2 loss. Chainsaw McKenzer had his own group of fans bunched together in the stands. They were fond of making chainsaw noises whenever they wanted McKenzer to cut somebody down on strikes.

For the first three innings, Chainsaw McKenzer gave his fans plenty to buzz about. Fulton's big pitcher whiffed eight of the first eleven batters he faced. Robbie was one of the strikeouts. Batting fifth, he was cut down on three straight fast balls. José Sanchez, Riverton's cleanup hitter, managed only a dribble grounder to the shortstop. He was easily tossed out at first. The other Tigers did no better. So far, Riverton was hitless.

The only good news for the Tigers was that they were holding the Bucks scoreless, too. Eagle Wilson was nipping the inside corner just the way Robbie knew he could. He had four strikeouts in the first three innings. And he finished out the top of the fourth inning with two more, bringing his total to six. The guys playing in the field behind Eagle scooped up everything else.

The bottom of the fourth inning started out as almost a repeat of the previous three. McKenzer struck out the first Tiger batter, then got José to hit a line drive back to the mound. There were two quick outs.

Robbie stepped up to the plate and settled into his batting stance. His back elbow was up, and his bat was perpendicular to the ground. Chainsaw looked in for the catcher's signal. Then Robbie was shocked to see him actually curl his upper lip and bare his teeth. He let out a low, throaty growl. *Oh, give me a break, Chainsaw!* thought Robbie. He stepped out of the box.

The umpire called time just as McKenzer had begun his pitching motion. Chainsaw was not happy with having to stop his motion. He gave an agonized bellow as he stopped. Then he stomped around the mound a little. After that, he started giving Robbie a look that made Mosely's glare seem downright friendly. *He's trying to draw all my attention away from the ball!* thought Robbie.

Once more, Robbie settled into the batter's box. He was determined to focus on the ball, not McKenzer's menacing stare. Robbie could hear Coach Franklin and his teammates, except for Mosely, calling out "Come on, Robbie!" and other encouragement. He even heard his mother yell "Cream it, Robbie boy!" Robbie imagined his father was just sitting there quietly, a little perplexed by all the commotion around him.

For the second time that day, Robbie didn't exactly hear McKenzer's first pitch whiz by for a strike. In fact, he didn't exactly *see* it very well, either. *This guy is fast! Fastest I've ever seen!*

Robbie stepped out of the box, even though Chainsaw gave the impression he would hate him even more for doing so. Taking a deep breath, Robbie saw Coach Franklin give him the hit-away sign. He stepped back in for the second pitch. It was another blur! Robbie lurched back. This time, he *did* hear a buzz—for the ball went very close to his ear! McKenzer was brushing Robbie back, trying to unnerve him.

A jolt of adrenaline went through Robbie's body. He regained his balance and set up for the next pitch. His nerves were thrumming with the sense of danger Chainsaw instilled. Robbie was alert, ready. He moved even closer to the plate, knowing that McKenzer could not resist a dare.

Sure enough, the Fulton hurler played some more "chin music." The pitch came in high and tight. But Robbie was waiting on it. He stepped into the ball early and swung. Robbie pulled the ball sharply down the third-base line. It went foul—but not by much.

With the count now at two strikes, one ball, Robbie had dug a deep hole for himself. He knew that favored the pitcher. But Robbie sensed a change in McKenzer. For the first time all day, he looked a little rattled. What was meant to be a brush-back pitch had just been knocked hard, though foul.

Chainsaw revved up for his next pitch. With the loudest grunt yet, he threw a burning fast ball right down the middle. Robbie took a huge swipe at it. *Whack!* He hit just underneath the pitch, sending it high into deep center field. The Fulton center fielder raced back and caught it about five yards in front of the fence.

As Robbie returned to the bench, he thought, *Stupid pitch! The guy has two strikes and one ball on me, with two outs, and he gives me something to hit. I think ol' Chainsaw is beginning to crack.*

In the fifth inning, the Bucks started getting to Eagle Wilson. He walked the leadoff batter, Raoul Spivey. Mojo had said Spivey was a well-known diver in local swimming competitions. Spivey was a definite stealing threat, and he took a confident lead off first. He didn't run on the first pitch, which was a ball. Robbie considered calling for a pitchout, feeling Spivey would surely steal on the second pitch. But that would put Eagle too far behind in the count. So Robbie called for a cross-seam fast ball, which tended to rise and was easier to catch and throw to second.

Sure enough, Spivey ran with the pitch. The ball came in high, too high for a strike, but Robbie had no time for disappointment. He fired a nice peg to second, low and on the bag. Jonesy caught it cleanly and put it down where Spivey could slide into it.

But Spivey didn't slide! He leapt *up* three feet over Jonesy's waiting tag and in midair performed a kind of half-gainer dive. Jonesy couldn't believe it! He just gaped as Spivey flew past. The Fulton runner landed on the other side of the bag, untagged. Then he reached back and touched the bag with his index finger. Safe.

The Fulton bench, of course, exploded. The Buck players jumped up cheering and whooping with laughter. One shouted out, "Nice slide, Raoul!" Another yelled out, "What's the matter, Luther? Don't you know where to put a tag?"

Robbie wondered if he should call time to calm down Eagle and let things quiet down a bit. He was still thinking about it when Mojo Johnson lifted up his hand to the base umpire, who called "Time." Gesturing for Robbie to join him at the mound, Mojo went over to talk with Eagle. Mojo, his shoulder pressed against Eagle's, said in a low voice, "Pretty amazing."

The three just stood there, saying nothing for a while. The hoots and yells from the Bucks were getting fewer and not as loud. Mojo caught Robbie's eye and ticked his head in Eagle's direction. *He wants me to say something to Eagle.*

Robbie didn't know what to say. He had no choice but to wait for something to occur to him.

"Um, Eagle, just so that hot-dog on second doesn't steal our on-base signals, we should go over them."

"I know what they are. You know what they are. Just use them! We don't have to go over them!"

"Right," said Robbie, a little flustered.

"Take it easy, Eagle," said Mojo. "It's one stolen base, not the whole game. Be cool. Nobody's

106

scored yet. Let's just try to keep their diver in shallow water at second, okay?" Mojo winked at Robbie.

"Sure, Mojo, sure!" snorted Eagle. "Let's just get on with it!"

"No outs!" Mojo called to the team, as he and Robbie headed back to their positions. *I should have yelled that,* thought Robbie. *It's the catcher's job to yell the number of outs to everyone. So many things to remember!* And now he had to remember exactly how his signals were changed with a man on second.

It was a complicated code. Coach Franklin had even invented a catcher's drill to help him learn it. He had to recite the code out loud for five minutes every practice. Robbie did this in a catcher's crouch while giving the corresponding signals. Still, in the excitement of his first starting game, he felt a little shaky in the memory department. *Let's see. I want him to throw a cutter fast ball. That's normally a three, but the count is even, so it's the* third *signal I flash.* Robbie flashed: one, two, three. *There, that wasn't so hard.*

Eagle shook him off.

Oh, no. What's he want? A curve? Robbie flashed: one, three, four.

When Eagle shook this sign off, Robbie felt like calling out, "What do you want? Just tell me!" Instead, he flashed: two, four, one. *Ah, he likes it. Cross-seam fast ball it is!*

The pitch came in slower than usual for an

Eagle fast ball. Then, at the last split second, it veered and dipped, scooting under Robbie's glove. Robbie tore after it. *The runner is surely going to third. He may even make it home if I don't catch up with that sucker!* Robbie finally got his hand on the ball and pivoted around. He saw Eagle where he should be, covering home. Robbie threw him a neat one-bouncer, and Spivey decided to stay at third.

"Nice catch, Belmont," Eagle snapped.

"I called for a cross-seam fast ball, not a curve."

"It's the second signal you give when the batter is ahead in the count!"

"The count was even. No balls, no strikes. That was the first pitch you threw to that guy."

"Never mind!" Eagle said, stomping back to the mound.

And I'll probably get charged for the passed ball, too! Robbie thought, trudging back to his dusty catcher's box. *All right. Man on third, signals back to normal.* Then Robbie flashed one through five, but Eagle shook off each one! *What's left to signal?* Robbie wondered in a mild panic. He flashed five again. Eagle was about to shake it off. Then he sighed nastily, wound up, and threw the change-up.

The batter was fooled a little. But the pitch was slow enough that he had time to hang in there and loft an easy fly ball to José Sanchez in center field. José's "I got it!" could be heard by everyone in the park.

Spivey, the diving base runner, was tagging

up at third. Leaning forward, he had his left foot on the edge of the bag. He was looking back at the ball falling toward José.

Caught! Spivey took off from third. Robbie had already whipped his mask off and straddled the third-base line a foot and a half from the plate. José's throw headed home. The ball grew from a tiny pill to a hulking white ball. Spivey slid between Robbie's legs, and the ball thumped into the catcher's mitt. Too late by a hair. The score was now 1–0, Fulton.

The score stayed the same for the next three and a half innings. Eagle recovered from the lone run scored on him and pitched well again. Chainsaw, however, was still blazing fast balls by Riverton batters. Robbie was the exception. After striking out and flying out to deep center field, he rapped a sharp double into right field. But he was left stranded on second base.

It was now the bottom of the ninth inning— last chance for the home team. Robbie was up first. *A hit, even a walk, could start a rally,* he thought. He dug in at the plate. "Come on, Robbie!" he could hear his mother shout from the bleachers. Riverton fans and players were all shouting encouragement now.

Chainsaw had no intention of letting anyone get on base. His first pitch was a fast ball, low and away. Robbie swung, hitting nothing but air. Fans of the Bucks whooped with joy. "Yo, batter, you swing like a rusty gate!" came one cry. "I felt that breeze from here, kid!" came another.

Trying to block out the noise, Robbie concentrated as hard as he could. McKenzer's next pitch broke inside and kneecap high. Robbie was too eager, getting around on it early and chipping it foul. Once more, he was in a deep hole. The count was two strikes, no balls.

As he got set for the third pitch, Robbie saw Chainsaw shake off two signals from the catcher. *Normally, a pitcher with an 0-2 count will throw some fishballs out of the strike zone,* thought Robbie. *But ol' Chainsaw doesn't want to! None of that wimpy tricky stuff for him! I'll bet he's going to try to blow another fast ball by me! This guy never learns!*

Chainsaw did as Robbie thought he would. And Riverton's catcher socked the fast ball deep in the gap between the left and center fielders. Tiger fans were on their feet as Robbie tore around the bases. The throw from the center fielder came too late for a tag at third. Robbie slid in safely for a triple.

No outs and a man on third—this was Riverton's best chance to tie the game, maybe win it. But the next two Tiger batters went down on strikes. And the last batter hit a line drive that was speared in the air by the second baseman. Robbie was left stranded on base again. No one could bring him home.

The Riverton Tigers had lost their first game. The only run scored came from a half-gainer and a wild pitch some thought was a passed ball by an inexperienced catcher.

After the game, Robbie heard Eddie Mosely talking to his friends in the locker room. "Eagle said the sacrifice fly that scored the run was hit because Belmont didn't call the right signal. Eagle said he shook off the cutter sign the first time, hoping Belmont would repeat it to confuse the batter. But Belmont didn't know beans about repeating signs!"

My career as a catcher is off to a shaky start, thought Robbie.

Mojo came over and clapped him on the shoulder. Under his breath, Mojo said, "When it's a strikeout, the pitcher is terrific. When it's a hit, the catcher called the wrong pitch. It can be a dry life behind the iron mask, Robbie. But hang in there. It has its rewards."

"Gentlemen," spoke up Coach Franklin, "I wished you could have gotten some more hits off Mr. McKenzer, but you still played a good game. That flip dive into second was the goofiest thing I ever saw in my life! Bad breaks, gentlemen. They happen.

"But the test of champions, you know, is not only how well they win, but also how well they lose. Don't let this loss get you down! It's only the first game of the season. We have a lot more left to play. With harder work, we'll win our fair share of them. So chin up! I'll see you all at practice tomorrow."

In the parking lot, Ralph Butler had joined up

with Brian Webster, Joshua Kenny, and Melinda Clark. They all greeted Robbie and tried to cheer him up. They reminded him that in his first varsity game, he had gone two for four, hitting a double and triple. Together, they laughed and shook their heads at the amazing diving steal. They also remarked on McKenzer's ferocious pitching.

As they were piling into Brian's station wagon, Eagle Wilson walked over. Cynthia Wu was with him. She was wearing a long white dress. Robbie noticed everything about her. She smiled at him, making him blush.

"Robbie, I'm sorry about that pitch that got away," said Eagle. "It was my fault. I messed up the signals. The steal by Spivey must have upset me more than I knew. I told the coach. He was surprised. Thanks for not saying anything."

"No problem, Eagle. Hey, you pitched a great game today."

"And you called a great game today, Robbie. See you."

Cynthia sang out a soft "Good night" with a friendly smile, as she and Eagle walked away.

Good things happen around Cynthia Wu, Robbie thought, gazing after her and Eagle.

"Let's get going," said Melinda, taking a seat next to Joshua and Ralph in the back of the station wagon. Robbie climbed in front with Brian. "That Cynthia Wu seems nice," Melinda said as Brian started the motor.

"She is," said Robbie, then wondered if he

had maybe agreed too quickly. "I mean, I've only met her a few times. But she is ... she's nice."

"Who's nice?" asked Brian.

"Cynthia Wu, that girl with Eagle," said Joshua.

"She *is* nice!" said Brian, waiting for an opening in the traffic.

"If anyone uses the word 'nice' again," shouted Melinda, "I'm going to be anything but!"

"That Cynthia Wu sure is wonderful," said Ralph, chuckling. Then he got serious. "She's one more friend we should have here. But you can't win them all, eh Robbie?"

"Not today, anyway," Robbie said without turning around.

"I hear you," said Ralph.

Chapter Thirteen

As the season progressed, Robbie grew more comfortable behind home plate. Whether he liked it or not, he was turning into a fine backstopper.

But there were days when catching got Robbie down. Lunging in the dirt for wild pitches wasn't a lot of fun. Long innings squatting behind the plate made his knees ache and his legs sore. He also didn't like batting with rubbery legs. A couple of times, he was barreled into and knocked over by runners trying to score. To top it all off, he suffered two dislocated fingers on vicious foul tips. Robbie winced when the coach popped them back in place before getting Robbie to a doctor.

Robbie never complained, though. He knew the aches and pains came with the position. He just had to play with them. Besides, it wouldn't do for a catcher to complain about every knock and nick. Pitchers could get away with that. And Robbie often had to make them feel better while he was suffering from some pain that made the pitcher's pale by comparison.

Eagle Wilson was a good example. Before every game, some part of his arm was "feeling funny" or "twinging." Or he had a cold coming on or hay fever. One time, he even said he had a disease that was eating away at his pitching arm! "Aw," Robbie would say to him, "too bad. You're a real trooper to pitch with such pain, Eagle. Maybe I should ask the coach to pitch someone else?"

Eagle may have liked to complain, but he liked to pitch even more. He hated to be taken out of a ball game, and Robbie knew it. Suggesting a replacement for Eagle always made him shake off his "hurt" and continue pitching.

After their opening loss to the Fulton Bucks, the Riverton Tigers went on a winning streak. This was mainly due to the hitting of José, Mojo, Jonesy, and Robbie. It was also due to the tough pitching of Eagle and to the constantly improving pitching of Wire and the short-relief hurler, Earl Markley. Wire and Robbie had each put on ten pounds since the season began.

Robbie usually played most if not all of the games. Coach Franklin would spell him for periods with Eddie Mosely and sometimes Tug Peters. Much as his bones creaked from catching, Robbie hated to come out of a game. In this, he was like Eagle.

Once in a while, Coach Franklin put Robbie in the outfield to keep his bat in the lineup. But Robbie had a habit of running full force into the fence or bleachers. The second time he did this, Robbie thought he was just chasing a fly ball when this *fence post* got in the way. The ball went for a homer, and he blacked out for a few seconds.

When he came to, Robbie was lying on his back. Opening his eyes, he saw a bunch of worried faces peering down at him. Robbie put his hand to his cheek and pulled it back. Blood! That's when he heard Jim Nelson, the right fielder, ask, "Is he going to die?" *Thanks, Nelson! Just what I wanted to hear!*

The cut on his cheek required stitches. When it healed, it left a small scar. Robbie would have to describe that scar for the rest of his life whenever a form asked, "Any identifying marks?" Coach Franklin never played Robbie in the outfield again. "You're too hard on the fences," he told Robbie.

That was fine with Robbie. At first, he thought he'd like playing outfield. It was like a trip to the country after working in the city all week. But even though his spikes were in green grass, Robbie's mind was still behind a mask in the catcher's box. He kept yelling how many outs there were after every out until José Sanchez and Jim Nelson started shushing him. In the wide open spaces of the outfield, he grew restless and itchy. When he returned to catching, it was like coming home.

The team's winning streak was attracting more and more media attention. The Riverton Tigers entered the last third of the season with a record of fourteen wins and one loss. Mainly because of his batting, Robbie picked up his share of publicity. Local sportswriters touted him as "the frosh sensation" or "the freshman of the year."

Around school, everybody knew Robbie's name. When walking down the street, people he never saw before would call out "Way to go, Robbie!" He knew what it was like to be a fan, because he was such a major-league fan himself. And it was flattering when someone would try to impress Robbie or give him instant trust because of his baseball reputation. Still, he felt something was missing in his baseball life.

After baseball practice one day, Robbie met up with Ralph Butler near the track. He had just finished his workout. Together, the two friends headed home. Robbie decided to tell Ralph how he felt.

"I know I have no reason to be down, Ralph," Robbie began. "I know I'm lucky to be playing varsity baseball as a freshman ... lucky to be a starter, too. And I hate it when people mope for no good reason, so I feel bad even telling you how down I am. But I am! I don't want to get up in the morning. Get this: I don't even want school to end because that means it's time for baseball practice! I shouldn't be depressed, but I am. This has never happened to me before, and I hate it."

"I have periods like that, too," said Ralph, "just like you're talking about. Weeks on end when I can hardly get myself to tie the laces on my track shoes. I'm glad this is only your first time. If it helps, I'm with you. All your friends are."

"Thanks, Ralph."

"And maybe it isn't just baseball or catching that's getting you down. Maybe it's something else, something you don't have."

"Like?"

Ralph didn't answer right away. They were walking down a quiet street, their equipment bags swinging at their sides. Then Ralph said softly, "Like Cynthia Wu."

Robbie started to make a joking reply to Ralph's remark. But then he saw Ralph wasn't buying it. The two friends walked on in silence.

When they came to Ralph's house, Robbie said, "But Cynthia is going with someone. Not just someone, but our best pitcher. A guy known to get jealous real fast. And she's a sophomore and I'm just a freshman."

"I think you're still allowed to say more than five words a week to her."

"I . . . I guess so."

"Take care, Robbie. Feel better real soon."

"I'll try. Thanks again, Ralph. I mean it."

Ralph smiled as he opened his front door. "Later, dude."

"Yeah, later."

Chapter Fourteen

The last game of the regular season for Riverton was against the Monsey Pirates. They had already lost once to the Tigers and were seeking revenge. A good team with a deep bench, the Pirates rocked Riverton's pitching for five runs. Robbie Belmont, nursing very sore knees, had to sit this game out. His bat was missed in the lineup, as the Tigers could come up with only one run. Still, they had won their division, finishing ahead of Monsey.

The real surprise of the league, however, was in the other division. The Jefferson City Chiefs had upset the Fulton Bucks twice during the regular season. Nearly perfect in the field, the Chiefs were a smart, scrappy team. They bunted well. They also hit a lot of singles, stole a high percentage of bases, and had a .304 team batting average. Short on power but long on patience, the Chiefs wore down their opponents. They completed the regular season with the best overall record in the league.

The Saturday of the league championship game

between Riverton and Jefferson City came faster than Robbie expected. Only a week had gone by since the last game of the regular season. But it was enough for Robbie's knees to recover. The pain was almost gone now, and Robbie had iced them before arriving at the ball field. There, in the parking lot, he met up with Eagle Wilson and Cynthia Wu.

"Hi, Eagle. Hi, Cynthia."

Eagle very carefully offered his hand. Robbie shook it and asked, "How's the arm?"

"Some twinges here in the shoulder, a numb spot on my forearm, but my fingers aren't cramping as much. How're the knees?"

"Pretty good. I shouldn't have any trouble with them today." Then, trying to feel less awkward, Robbie said, "Guess we both have our share of war wounds, huh?"

Eagle ignored Robbie's last remark. "Hey, there's Mojo! Yo, Mojo, wait up!" Eagle grabbed his bag and, without looking back, trotted ahead to his old catcher.

Robbie and Cynthia smiled at each other. Robbie picked up his bag, and they started to walk slowly toward the locker room. Robbie had gotten up enough courage to talk more to Cynthia over the last few weeks. She was as easy to be with as she had been the first time they met in the library.

"How are you?" she asked.

Usually, that question merely pushed an automatic playback button in Robbie that said, "Fine.

120

How are you?" But when Cynthia asked it, he took it seriously.

"I'm okay. I just seem kind of tired of baseball."

"Not a good way to be right before an important baseball game!"

"Guess not."

"I'll watch you more than usual today, for whatever that's worth."

"It's worth."

"What?"

"A lot."

"Oh?" She raised her eyebrows and smiled. Robbie smiled back. Then, waving, he disappeared into the locker room.

The stands were packed solid with fans of both teams. Everyone there knew what was at stake. The winner would go on to play for the county championship. It had been seven years since the Tigers last played in a county championship. And that one they lost.

Coach Franklin was clapping his hands a lot and pacing eagerly around to the players in the locker room. He wanted the league title very much, and all the players knew it. But he was also worried. Monsey had hit Riverton's pitching hard last week. The coach just hoped his team had shaken off that loss by now.

Watching Coach Franklin get psyched for the game was enough to get his players psyched, too. Robbie felt especially alert today. The aches and pains had faded. He was ready, if a little tight.

"Gentlemen," spoke up the coach, extending his hand, palm down. All the players huddled around him, placing hands on top of his. "Let's bring back the league title to Riverton!" With a loud, resounding "Ho!" the huddle broke. The doors to Riverton's locker room flew open, and out poured the Tigers onto the field. Their fans were on their feet, cheering at the top of their lungs.

When the Chiefs came out onto the field a few moments later, they received the same noisy welcome from their fans. Then, after a brief period of warming up, the game began. The first three innings were relatively quiet. Each team got two singles. Robbie threw out one Jefferson City player trying to steal second. It was a dead-on throw, surprising the runner sliding in. After that, the Chiefs tried no more steals for a while.

Robbie was mildly amazed that every Chief tucked the bottom of his pin-striped uniform pants exactly one inch below his knees. The beaks of the Chiefs' caps seemed to be curved the same way, too. Jefferson City was a team known for close discipline, for following set patterns. They were almost machinelike. That's why they were so successful.

Robbie went hitless his first two times at bat. The first time up, he slammed a liner. The third baseman dove to his right, and his glove swallowed the ball with a popping sound. Robbie was further irked when the third baseman called for a time-out to brush off his uniform.

Robbie wanted to do something sensational the second time up, but the pitcher gave him nothing but low and outside sinkers, and low and inside fishballs. With the count two balls and one strike, Robbie swung halfheartedly at a bad high pitch. The ball popped lazily to the center fielder for a routine out. The pep that had filled Robbie in the locker room was fading fast.

After the center fielder made the catch, Robbie trotted in from the base path and noticed Cynthia looking at him. She was looking at him plainly, with no judgment on her face. *Oh, yes,* thought Robbie, *she said she would watch me more than usual. Too bad for her.*

But as the game went on, he became more and more aware of her attention. Every time he glanced in her direction, Robbie knew she saw him looking. *She really is watching me. I could probably talk about any play with her after the game.* Gradually, Robbie found himself standing a little straighter and trying to avoid anything that Cynthia might think was sloppy or lazy. He didn't seem to be getting more tired as the game went on, but more energetic.

Coach Franklin's voice was getting hoarse from shouting encouragement. The Tigers scratched out a run in the fifth inning. Jim Nelson blooped a single to short center field. A sacrifice bunt moved him to second. The coach then had a talk with Eagle, the next batter. On the first pitch, Eagle squared around to bunt. The third baseman ran in. But instead of letting the ball hit the bat, Eagle gave a little choked-up swing at the ball. It dribbled untouched past the startled third baseman.

Nelson had run for third base as soon as the third baseman ran in for the bunt. The ball puttered to a stop at the grass edge of the outfield. The shortstop raced for it, and Nelson did not stop at third. Coach Franklin, who was also Riverton's third-base coach, waved Nelson on frantically. The coach's voice was raspy from shouting to Nelson to keep running.

Like a runaway freight train, Nelson lumbered homeward. The shortstop skittered to the ball, picked it up neatly, and took a second to get perfect balance before throwing the ball. That balancing second, sensible and picturesque as it was, gave Nelson the time he needed to make it to the catcher before the ball. The catcher went head over heels, and the ball bounced off his shoulder. He and Nelson tumbled over home plate together. The Tigers were ahead, 1–0.

Coach Franklin clapped and croaked hoorays from his spot near third base. Eagle preened and looked noble on first base. He called grandly for his jacket, as if his arm would freeze up without it. The temperature was in the high seventies.

The score stayed 1–0 until the eighth inning. Robbie led off. He stepped into the batter's box feeling a strange sense of anticipation. For the last few innings, he'd been more aware that Cynthia Wu was watching him. But her look was so mild that it didn't distract him. And it made Robbie more aware of what he was doing. He was right in the rhythm of the game.

124

The name of the Chiefs' pitcher was Gantner. He stood six feet tall and had a good assortment of pitches. More important, he knew how to mix them up. Every pitch he threw was tough to hit. Gantner heaved in a sinking fast ball that went by Robbie for a strike. The next pitch was a curve that came in almost as fast. It broke down and away at the end. Robbie had seen a few of those curves today. He read this one like a new friend, stroking it cleanly over Gantner's head for a single.

Robbie rounded first base carefully. The center fielder had fielded the hit and was already returning the ball to the infield. Robbie noticed Cynthia applauding happily as he hurried back to first. Doctor Leo Roberts, Riverton's trainer and first-base coach, gave him two thumbs up and said, "Way to start it off, Robbie."

And start it off he did. The Tigers woke up from their slumber. Suddenly, this league championship game began looking like Tiger batting practice. Everyone hit. Mojo hit a soft lob off the handle of his bat. The ball sailed over the third baseman's head. José banged the first pitch down the third-base line for a double. Jonesy swatted one down the right-field line. Nelson hit one off the end of his bat that squibbed past the first baseman's glove. Run after run scored. Riverton was now up, 6–0!

For the first time all year, Jefferson City's well-oiled machine broke down. Shocked by the five runs Riverton scored in the eighth inning, the

Chiefs tried to catch up in a hurry. They took chances, and they made errors. Lacking long-ball hitters, Jefferson City was in a bind. No matter how hard they tried, they came up empty.

Robbie's last time at bat, in the ninth inning, was a dinker back to the pitcher. In four trips to the plate, all he could manage was a single. But it had started off the Tigers' eighth-inning rally. He felt good about that.

The game ended on a pop foul that Robbie ran down and caught just off to the left of the backstop. The final score was 6–0. With the ball still in his mitt, Robbie rushed toward the mound. There, his teammates were already mobbing Eagle. The Tiger hurler had thrown a shutout to win the league championship. Even Coach Franklin and Doctor Roberts were clapping each other on the back. Riverton fans streamed out on the field, whooping for joy.

The next week, Riverton's hottest news item was the Tigers' upcoming county championship against the Bay High Colts and their star pitcher, Tyrone Hightower. Photographers and reporters attended every Tiger practice. Robbie was interviewed three times and was on the local TV news for about five seconds. The reporter asked him who would win the county championship. Robbie answered, "We will, of course!" He watched it with his parents. His mother applauded and squealed with delight. His father said Robbie "certainly looked convinced" that the Tigers would win.

Riverton High School gave its baseball team a huge pep rally the Friday before the county championship. All classes were canceled for the last period. The cheerleaders put on a tumbling and acrobatic show to the school band's booming music. The rafters of the crowded auditorium started to shake under the heavy stomping, clapping, and singing. The team stood shuffling quietly outside the auditorium door, waiting for their entrance cue. And suddenly it came! Cynthia Wu called out over the microphone, "And here they are, the next county champions, our very own Riverton Tigers!"

The door was pulled open, and the team came out in more or less single file, bumping into each other frequently. They lined up across the stage, peering out at the standing ovation they were getting. Some players merely smiled. Others waved. And still others made some exaggerated gestures that got good laughs. Robbie basically stood still and tried to look pleasant. Later, Melinda told him he seemed to be scowling the whole time.

Chapter Fifteen

The county championship game was played in Grout Memorial Stadium. Though the parking lot was huge, Robbie was able to cross paths again with Cynthia and Eagle.

"Hi, Eagle. Hi, Cynthia."

"Hi, Robbie," said Cynthia. Eagle gave a small nod, then sighed and looked into space.

"What's the weather report on your arm today?" Robbie asked.

"I can't get my wrists loose."

"Shake them out. Like this." Robbie put his bag down and started shaking his hands as if he had burned them. Cynthia laughed and started shaking her hands wildly, too. With a low moaning sigh, Eagle put his bag down and started shaking his hands. He looked like the conductor of some bizarre symphony. After ten shakes, Eagle stopped suddenly and said, "That's not helping." He started looking around. Then he said, "Hey, there's Mojo!" And just as he did the week before, Eagle rushed off without looking back.

Robbie and Cynthia both had their hands held out in front of them. They smiled at each other and lowered their arms. Robbie picked up his bag. They started walking toward the players' entrance. Neither of them spoke for a while. Finally, Cynthia broke the silence.

"Would you do me a favor in today's game?" she asked.

Robbie was momentarily surprised. "Sure, Cynthia. What?"

"Show me how great a baseball player you can be. Play the greatest game of your life."

The idea sounded good to Robbie. "I'll try," he said, smiling.

A stiff breeze suddenly blew through the parking lot. Cynthia reached over and brushed back the hair that had fallen over Robbie's forehead. She did it so gently, so softly, that Robbie blushed. This, in turn, made Cynthia blush.

"Uh, hope it doesn't get too windy for the game," said Robbie. He couldn't think of anything else to say.

"It's just a short gust," she said. After a pause, Cynthia looked straight at Robbie. "I like you, Robbie Belmont."

"Same here, Cynthia," said Robbie. "I mean, you know, I like you, too."

"Good," she said, smiling. Cynthia looked away for a moment, then back at Robbie. "Remember what I said in the library about sort of being able to read minds? Like it's a natural thing?"

"Yes."

"Well, I think you can do that as a catcher with the hitters. They give clues to what they're expecting."

"Okay. I'll keep that in mind."

"Okay. Have a great game, then. The greatest!"

"Thanks."

Robbie walked quickly through the players' entrance. Uniformed attendants stood around, but the atmosphere was still casual. Brian greeted him and checked his name off on a clipboard. A doorman let him through to the locker room. Inside, there were more attendants, neat stacks of clean towels, rubdown tables, whirlpool baths, large lockers, and cushioned benches. *Something like baseball heaven*, thought Robbie.

The conversation with Cynthia still echoed in Robbie's head. *Have a great game? I sure hope so. And what was Cynthia saying about reading batters' minds? It seemed clear when I was with her. But now ...* Robbie felt like Alice in Wonderland right after she drank that potion. He didn't know if it would cause huge growth or great shrinkage.

Coach Franklin had a little surprise for the Tigers. A few minutes before they were ready to leave the locker room, he brought in a baseball friend to say a few words. Robbie recognized the tall, impressive figure instantly.

"Gentlemen," the coach said, the tone of his voice calling for quiet, "I'd like to introduce Eddie Trent!"

Eddie looked relaxed, even though he and the New York Titans were in the middle of a tight pennant race. Eddie was batting .321 this year. He was also hitting more home runs than ever before and was chief caretaker of a pitching staff that was the envy of both major leagues. Robbie,

130

after a season of catching, knew that Trent had a lot to do with the success of the Titans this year.

"Coach Franklin asked me to stop by and say a few words," Eddie began, "and we all know how persuasive the coach can be." Eddie smiled at the coach, and a few players chuckled. "All I want to tell you is play hard, have fun out there, and don't quit. No matter what. If you do all that, the final score won't matter. Because you'll be winners anyway. So good luck! And win this one for Coach Franklin!"

The Tigers stood and clapped. Eddie Trent patted Coach Franklin on the back, then raised a clenched victory fist to the team. There was more hollering. A chant began: "Coach, Coach, Coach!" Pretending to be hard of hearing, Coach Franklin cupped his ear. "What was that? I'm sorry. Could you all repeat that again a bit louder?" "COACH, COACH, COACH!" everyone screamed.

Eddie Trent came over and clapped Robbie on the back. With the coach smiling over his shoulder, Eddie spoke to Robbie *catcher to catcher*! "I haven't forgotten that diving catch you made off me in the outfield. Now you're behind the iron mask yourself, I see! How do you like it?"

"I like it more and more," Robbie answered.

"Coach Franklin says you have the knack for it. Anything I can do to help, just let me know. I won't be far from the dugout."

"Thanks, Mr. Trent."

" 'Mr. Trent'? Call me Eddie. After all, we catchers have to stick together."

Robbie smiled. "All right . . . Eddie."

"That's better."

Eddie looked intently into Robbie's face. *Must be the kind of look he gives a pitcher to see if he should be taken out of the game or not!* Eddie just kept looking at Robbie for a while, and Robbie felt a quiet fire move up his spine. *I think the coach may have told Eddie about my less-than-peppy mood lately.*

Eddie spoke again. "Remember what I wrote on that ball I gave you a while back?"

Robbie nodded. He'd never forget it: "Great catch, kid! You came to play!"

Eddie turned very serious. "The difference between talent and achievement is mental. All the skill in the world won't matter if you're not ready, not alert, not thinking. That's what 'coming to play' means." The smile now returned to Eddie's face. "Have a great one, kid!"

"Thanks, Eddie."

"Gentlemen!" Coach Franklin called out. "Let's go win that county title!"

With a roar, the Riverton Tigers charged out of the locker room and onto the field. They were greeted by a roar much louder than their own. Grout Memorial Stadium was ringing with the sound of baseball fans.

Melinda and her stat sheets were close to the Tiger dugout. Coach Franklin had taken her and Brian to scout the Bay High Colts' last two games. Robbie had been studying their reports on the Colts' batters all week. He wasn't thrilled to

132

learn that Bay High had six batters in the starting lineup hitting over .300. Nor was Robbie happy that these same Colt hitters were particularly fond of fast balls—Eagle's bread-and-butter pitch! But he was able to memorize the strengths and weaknesses each batter had.

Cynthia was sitting next to Melinda. When Robbie looked over, Cynthia was looking right at him. Melinda noticed, and a smile came over her face. *Melinda suspects*, Robbie thought. Ralph sat next to Melinda, smiling broadly. *Ralph definitely knows! He knew before anyone*. Robbie's parents were sitting higher in the stands, next to Joshua's parents.

Robbie turned away from gazing at the crowd. He had some ball to play. If he was going to play his best, he had to start now.

Robbie took batting practice. There was no lazy swinging of the weighted bat for him this time. *Concentrate! The right move wants to happen. Let it. Get out of your own way*. He mentally scanned each part of his swing for even the smallest defect.

Robbie took his fifteen swings in the batter's box. He swung as if each pitch were being thrown to him in the ninth inning, with two outs, a count of 3–2, and the tying run on second. *And Cynthia is watching!* He kept seeing himself through her eyes, and what he saw looked pretty good! He was hitting the ball with sheer joy all over the place.

In a seat close to the Tiger dugout, and not far from Cynthia Wu, Eddie Trent was also watching

Robbie closely. Eddie's wide-open gaze gleamed a bit as it tracked Robbie's fluid, power-packed strokes. Robbie reminded the Titan star of his own high-school days, when his full power first started to emerge.

Robbie felt good, strong, and excited. There was one last batting practice pitch for Robbie. He launched it deep off the number 8, for eighth inning, on the scoreboard. His own number was 8. *I think we can call that a good sign!* Robbie thought. He turned and hustled back to the dugout, clapping his hands and chattering "Lotta hustle! Lotta hustle now!" His teammates gave brief surprised looks at their catcher, who for so long had been reserved and withdrawn. Then they responded with lively chatter themselves. Robbie picked up his catcher's mitt and jogged fast to the right-field bullpen to warm up Eagle Wilson.

Eagle barely acknowledged Robbie's arrival. He was standing on the bullpen rubber. Eagle was looking up at the blue sky while slowly rubbing his pitching wrist. His glove was wedged under his armpit.

"Yo, Eagle! How's the ol' wing? Feel like tossing some baseball, maybe? Good day for it."

"Right. Right." Eagle gave his wrist one last careful shake, sighed, and began tossing Robbie some warm-ups.

Robbie didn't bother to talk or chatter. Eagle had wrapped himself in his usual pre-game bubble, as if any outside input would interfere with his preplanned show. Gradually, his pitches picked up steam, and Robbie was able to get an idea of how Eagle would pitch that day. Although the fast ball had a moderate amount of kick, his accuracy would be his strongest asset this game. But it was a nervous accuracy, and his speed suffered. Robbie knew from experience he couldn't talk Eagle into throwing more freely. He could mention it to Mojo Johnson, who could sometimes break through Eagle's shell.

At the end of the warm-up, Eagle finally threw some pitches full speed. Again, they were not overpowering. But they chugged in nicely, right where Robbie put his target.

"Okay," said Eagle finally. "I'm ready." He said it as if the whole stadium had been waiting for him to make this announcement so the ball game could begin.

"Way to look!" called Robbie. "You're throwing the ball right where we want it today!"

"Right. Right," agreed Eagle, nodding gravely.

"See you in the dugout, Eagle," said Robbie, heading off. In the dugout, he talked with Mojo and Coach Franklin about how Eagle was throwing. Mojo said he'd try to get Eagle to free up his motion.

The two teams came out and stood on their respective foul lines. A local choir sang the national anthem with a lot of feeling. As their warm, strong voices soared with the line "o'er the land of the free," Robbie suddenly looked over his shoulder and saw Cynthia smiling at him. And as "the home of the brave" was sung, Robbie faced the mound again. He saw Eagle give him a puzzled look, then look suspiciously over his shoulder at Cynthia. *Uh-oh*, thought Robbie. The song ended, the crowd cheered, and the umpire yelled "Play ball!"

Chapter Sixteen

Robbie's first inkling he was going to have one of those magic days came when he threw his first warm-up to second. The toss went fast and with pinpoint accuracy. Jonesy whistled out loud from the infield. "Whoo-ee, Robbo! We'll keep the bases clean today with throws like that!" Everything seemed to be happening in a white light for Robbie. He had never felt this way before.

The first Bay High batter was a first-ball hitter, and he looked it. His name was Henry Morrison. But his teammates kept calling him Mad Dog. "Come on, Mad Dog!" they shouted. "Eat him up, Mad Dog!" He pawed the dirt in the batter's box. It seemed only a leash could keep him from running out and biting Eagle in the leg.

Melinda Clark was looking at a stat sheet on her lap. It showed that Mad Dog feasted on all fast balls. Robbie had carefully studied the sheet over the past few days. And he had already arranged for Eagle to throw a curve as his first pitch. Robbie gave Eagle the signal.

The second time Robbie got the feeling of magic

was when he caught that first curve dipping under Morrison's growling swing. The ball whammed into his mitt. He caught it with such ease that it didn't sting his hand. The ball felt perfectly sized and weighted. He noticed this particular ball had a slightly higher seam than usual. Robbie knew that all balls, new or not, had different features. *Higher seam helps a curve ball. Call for another curve.*

This time, however, Eagle shook him off. Robbie saw the batter's face change from a *fast ball* expression to a *curve* expression. So Robbie called for the cutter fast ball.

It worked like a charm. The batter *had* been expecting a curve. He swung late and weakly. *How did I know he was expecting a curve? What the heck is a curve expression anyway?* Then Robbie remembered Cynthia saying there were clues to reading minds. *You read minds by reading bodies,* he thought. Robbie looked at the batter again.

Mad Dog was studying Eagle's body for clues as hard as Robbie was studying his. *He's going to protect the plate. He'll bite at anything reachable.* Robbie called for a curve and offered a low, low outside target. *Fishball zone!* Mad Dog fished and missed; he was out on three straight pitches.

"One out!" Robbie called. His index finger was pointing to the sky from his raised hand. He felt like the Statue of Liberty holding up a torch. His voice rang through Grout Memorial Stadium. *Everything's going right,* he thought. *This is very unusual. I'm not sure what to do. I'm not used to it.* And in something like Cynthia's tone of voice, he thought, *Just do what you're doing. Because everything's going right!*

Robbie's reading of the next two batters and Eagle's continuing accuracy combined to get a ground out to Mojo and an infield fly that Jonesy ate like candy. It was Riverton's turn to bat.

In the dugout, the Tiger players patted Eagle on the back for a good first inning. He sat there giving a serious little nod to each compliment. Mojo sat next to Eagle for a spell. Robbie overheard Mojo compliment Eagle for "putting a little joy" on the last pitch he threw. In fact, it had been the pitch Eagle threw with the freest motion.

"How do you feel, Robbie?" asked Brian, handing him a towel.

"Super," Robbie said, wiping off the dirt and sweat that had already started to blacken his forearms and face. "I've never felt better in all my life."

Brian was happily surprised by Robbie's mood. "All right, Robbo! You're looking like yourself again!" Brian said. The two friends exchanged a low-five slap.

Robbie unbuckled his shin guards because he knew he would bat this inning. He'd been batting third in the lineup since the fifth game. Jonesy batted leadoff as he had ever since his sophomore year.

Bay High's pitcher came to the county championship game with a reputation ten miles long. He was the reason so many major-league scouts were sprinkled throughout the best seats in the stadium. Tyrone Hightower had a bagful of nicknames. Among them were High Power Hightower, Tyrone the Typhoon, and Power Man. He stood about six feet five inches tall, and he weighed two hundred ten pounds.

Melinda's scouting report mentioned that his curve was as strong as his scarifying fast ball. He was also likely to throw either one no matter what the count. Hightower threw what Mojo called a "heavy" ball. His fast balls tended to sink, and his curve "fell off the table like a shot-put."

Jonesy, batting leadoff, went down on three pitches. Robbie took his bat to the on-deck circle. Jonesy, passing on his way back to the dugout, said, "This guy makes McKenzer look like a pussycat!"

Robbie shuddered at the thought. The Fulton Bucks' Chainsaw McKenzer was the toughest pitcher he had ever faced. *Tough, but dumb*, thought Robbie. Hightower was obviously tough and smart.

Mojo Johnson batted second. He worked Hightower to a two-two count. Then Mojo watched a fast ball blow by. *Mr. Power Man put a little extra on that last one*, thought Robbie. Passing Robbie, Mojo muttered, "That guy would be fast even in slow motion!"

What's the big deal? thought Robbie. He stepped in the batter's box, smoothing the dirt out just right for his feet. *This guy's not shooting BBs.*

He's still throwing a baseball, right? A baseball I can hit.

Robbie wasn't thinking about anything but getting settled comfortably in the box. His hands were wrapped firmly around the thin handle of the bat.

Hightower peered in for the catcher's signal. His expression was neutral and businesslike. *He doesn't know anything about me as a hitter. No Melindas on their side! He just thinks of me as third in the lineup. Little does he know! It'll be a fast ball, of course.*

A fast ball it was, kicking and sinking toward Robbie's hands. Quick as a cat, Robbie stepped toward third and whipped the bat around. *Bam!* The fat of the bat caught the fat of the ball. The hit could be heard throughout the stadium. The crowd roared as the ball sailed higher and higher.

But then the crowd's "Ah!" became a disappointed "Oh!" as the ball shifted foul. It went high over the wall, but on the wrong side of the left-field foul pole. It was a very long strike.

Strangely, Robbie wasn't disappointed. He did not feel that he had only one or two long balls in his bat and that he had just wasted one. He simply made a slight adjustment in his stance.

Hightower caught the new ball the umpire tossed to him. As he rubbed it up, he gave Robbie a brief serious look. *That's right, Power Man! I'm no easy out!* Robbie smiled, startling Bay High's catcher a bit. Somehow, Robbie just knew that Hightower would come back with a curve.

Hightower went into his wind-up and released the ball. It was a curve, and Robbie was ready for it. With one huge swing, he ripped the ball high into left field. Mad Dog Morrison, the Colts' left fielder, never moved a muscle. There was no use running back to the wall for this one. It was a home run the moment it left the bat. Amazingly, the ball cleared not only the outfield wall, but the second, higher stone wall thirty yards behind it. Robbie had just hit the ball *out of the stadium*!

There was a second of stunned silence in the crowd, then a burst of wild cheering. Robbie could see his mother holding her hand against her forehead as he rounded the bases. Even she couldn't quite believe what she had just seen with her own eyes. José Sanchez had a big smile on his face as he waited for Robbie to cross the plate. "Awesome, man!" said José, giving Robbie two high fives. "Just awesome!" Other teammates pounded Robbie on the back as he jogged to the dugout. Even Coach Franklin was shaking his head on the dugout steps.

After the hoopla, Robbie started putting his gear on. Everyone leapt to their feet when José smashed a screamer down the third-base line. Bay High's third baseman took two leaping strides, and the ball screeched into the webbing of his glove. It was a fantastic catch—and the third out. "Anyway, this guy is hittable!" Robbie called out to his teammates. He picked up his iron mask and trotted to his position. The magic was getting to be more of a normal presence for him now.

Chapter Seventeen

Neither side got another man on base until the top of the third inning. That's when Mad Dog dribbled the first pitch, a fishball, back to the pitcher. Eagle Wilson fielded it cleanly and turned to throw to first. Suddenly, he jerked his hand with a scream, and the ball flew out of it. Jonesy scrambled to pick up the ball, but he had no chance to get the runner at first.

It was an error on the pitcher, who was now holding his hand out, trying to move it. Coach Franklin and Doctor Roberts dashed out to him. "It's some sort of cramp!" said Eagle, wincing in pain. "I can't move my wrist!"

Doctor Roberts gently moved the wrist. Eagle flinched and cried out. Josh Kenny came out with ice, which Eagle gratefully accepted. "We'd better take you out, Eagle," said the coach.

"Darn wrist!" said Eagle, leaving the mound with the ice pack pressed to his wrist. Coach Franklin called in Earl Markley to pitch.

Earl was a junior, just under six feet tall, whom Robbie and just about everyone liked. He had a harder fast ball than Eagle, but not very good control. His curve was good, but he had even less control over it than his fast ball. His change-up, a dinky sinker, wasn't half bad. But he didn't like to throw it. He only had confidence in his fast ball.

He threw his warm-ups from a stretch position, since he would start pitching with a man on base. Robbie ran out to discuss signals before the game resumed.

"Hi, Robbie."

"How do you feel, Earl?"

"Uh, pretty good. How do I look?"

"You're throwing real well, better than usual even. But the next five guys in their order eat fast balls for breakfast. So we'll be throwing more off-speed pitches than usual."

"Whatever you call, Robbie. You've always done fine by me."

"One, fast; two, curve; three, change?"

"Right."

Earl went into his man-on-base motion and peeked over at Morrison's long lead off first. He didn't like it one bit, and whirled and fired to Mojo. Mad Dog made it back by a fingernail. *You can tell a lot about a pitcher's personality from his pick-off action to first*, Robbie thought. Earl always went all out for the pick-off. He practiced his pick-off motion much more often than the team's other pitchers. He wouldn't allow a big lead off first. As a catcher, Robbie really appreciated this.

Mad Dog wasn't called Mad for nothing. He took an even longer lead, and Earl immediately hurled the ball knee high to Mojo. Mad Dog was safe this time only because he'd started back for the bag the instant he crossed the line he knew Earl was drawing. Morrison now took a reasonable lead. Earl threw to the plate, and Mad Dog bolted toward second. It was Robbie's turn to deal with him now. Markley had done his part.

In one smooth, quick motion, Robbie caught and threw the ball toward second base. It was a perfect toss. Jonesy caught it right where he could make the tag instantly. Mad Dog lunged headfirst toward the bag, his hands outstretched. It was no use. Jonesy made a clean tag. "You're out!" said the umpire near the play.

"One down!" Robbie called to all his fielders. He raised his finger once again like Liberty's torch. "One away!"

Then Earl Markley lost control. No matter where Robbie held his glove, no matter how many fast balls he called, the non-strikes kept pouring in. In two quick minutes, Earl had walked two straight. "One out!" Robbie called. "Force at third and second. Get two if you can!"

The Colts' cleanup hitter was their first baseman, a 250-pound all-state tackle from their football team. He had a blunt nickname: Meat. But he surprised everyone in the ballpark by laying a bunt down the third-base line. Earl Markley had to field it. Riverton's third baseman was John Roberts, the son of Doctor Roberts. John had to stay back in case of a force play at third.

Mojo Johnson had raced in from first as soon

as he saw Meat square off. It was going to be a close play wherever Earl threw it. It was the catcher's job to call where the throw should go. Mojo had been helping Robbie out with these calls all season. Now Mojo called "First base!" to Earl, who had just fielded the slow roller. A split second after Mojo's call, Robbie yelled "Third!"

Earl hesitated a moment, then whirled and fired to third. John Roberts stretched for the force-out catch on third. The ball was not a strike, but it didn't have to be. It beat the runner by a shoelace. Robbie's call had been tough, but correct. A throw to first would have been a sure out. But in a 1–0 ball game, keeping a runner off third was top priority. Robbie knew the Colts had a good chance at third. Still, he felt Markley could make the play.

"Good call, Robbo!" said Mojo, loud enough for the whole team to hear. "Sorry about making a call myself. Old catcher's habits die hard. It's all yours from now on."

"Two outs!" yelled Robbie to his team, holding up two fingers this time. "Force at third and second! Get the easy one if you can!" Robbie could feel the whole team listening to him. That last play marked a subtle but real shift in the team's attention on the field. In effect, Mojo had just handed over the team's leadership to Robbie.

The next Colt batter was Tyrone Hightower. A pitcher who could hit, he batted fifth, not ninth. But the play Earl made at third boosted his confidence. He brought his wildness under control enough to hurl three smokeballs. Each nicked a corner, and Hightower was called out on strikes. The score stayed at 1–0, Riverton.

Angry with himself for striking out, Hightower began the bottom of the third inning by pouring it on. Mojo barely managed to get a piece of his late-swinging bat on the ball. Meat, playing first base, caught the meager pop-up in foul territory. Robbie went up to the plate for the second time that day.

Hightower remembered him, all right. He remembered how Robbie had blasted each of the two pitches he got. Robbie could almost see Hightower's muscles bunch to put even more on his pitches than he had to Mojo.

Robbie's mind was clear of everything but the game at hand. He felt right in rhythm with how things were going. *I'm going to hit this one out of here, too,* he thought. As he looked out at Hightower, all sounds shrank. Robbie felt a deep calm within him.

Hightower's first pitch was a fast ball, high and inside. Robbie stepped back as it passed for ball one. He took his batter's stance in the box once more and waited. The second pitch Hightower threw him was a wicked curve nipping the lower outside part of the plate. Robbie now had one strike and one ball on him.

The rest of Riverton's lineup was not hitting, and Robbie now felt he had to come through with another homer. For the first time in the batter's box that day, he felt slightly untuned.

Hightower's next pitch was a curve bent low over the outside corner again. Robbie watched it, and the umpire called a loud "Stee-rike!"

Robbie stepped out of the box to get himself together. He hadn't been *in* that play. Instead, he'd been watching it from a little plastic shell like the one Eagle assumed before the game. Robbie took a deep breath and shook himself out of it.

This time, he stepped into the box with resolve. The high energy he'd been holding back now spilled over into movement. He dug a deeper gulley for his back foot, smoothed the area where his front foot would be striding, and took several sharp practice swings. The crowd started cheering, hoping for something spectacular again.

Hightower must have thought what worked twice would work again. He unleashed another low, outside curve.

Robbie was guessing change-up, not curve. Still, he got his bat swiftly around on the ball. Once more, it soared high into left field. Mad Dog drifted back, back, back, looking up calmly, waiting for the ball to drop. Then Mad Dog decided not to wait. He jumped up, catching his free hand on the top of the wall. Morrison started to pull himself up as if he were trying to escape a prison.

Everyone in the stadium could hear Mad Dog growl as he climbed. He made it to the top and stretched out his glove at the descending ball. It hit the topmost part of his webbing—then plopped out over the wall. Robbie had just hit his second home run! Riverton fans went wild! The score was upped to 2–0!

Chapter Eighteen

Hightower closed out the inning by whiffing the next two Tiger batters.

The pitchers' duel stayed at 2–0 until the seventh inning. Hightower kept mowing down Riverton batters. Earl Markley remained wild, leaving men on bases every inning. But he kept rallying to get the outs. In the top of the seventh, Earl loaded the bases with two walks and a hit batter. There were no outs. And the third man in Bay High's order, their catcher, was up. His teammates called him Big Foot.

"Nice hitting there, guy," he said to Robbie as he rubbed some dirt on his hands before stepping into the box.

"Thanks."

The Colt catcher was *huge*. His muscles bulged from lots of honest labor with weights. Yet his practice swings were surprisingly gentle.

I just want Earl to get the ball over! thought Robbie. He flashed the signal for a fast ball. Robbie offered a pumpkin pie of a target smack in the middle of the strike zone. He hoped Earl would at least come close to it.

It didn't happen. Earl's hand seemed to clutch the ball just as he should have been letting it go. The oddly released pitch angled nastily away to Robbie's right. It skidded in the dirt as Robbie threw himself at it. His shoulder thumped to the ground, and the ball bounced hard off his glove wrist. *Yeow!* he almost screamed.

Blocking out the pain, Robbie looked to his right, then to his left, and then to his right again. *Where's the ball? Where's the ball?* His mask cut off some of his side vision, so he whipped it off his head. *There it is!* It was right between his feet!

Robbie picked up the ball immediately. The runner on third base was only *thinking* about dashing for home. After all, the ball had been lying two inches from home plate. It was clear as daylight for everybody else in the stadium except the catcher. *Another fine trait of the position,* thought Robbie. *The acceptance of the occasional clown role.*

"Nice save," Big Foot said.

"I appreciate that," answered Robbie. "Especially from another catcher."

"You got it, man."

The umpire tossed out a clean ball to Earl as Robbie brushed himself off. Then he squatted back down behind the plate. He gave Earl the signal for a fast ball down the middle.

This time, the ball sailed five feet over Robbie's head. *One run will score at least,* thought Robbie, chasing after the wild pitch. It bounced all the way back against the backstop. The runner on second might even try for home. Robbie was huffing and puffing like mad, in a weird race with the Colt runner now making the turn at third.

Robbie finally caught up with the ball. Barehanding it, he turned and threw to the distant Markley covering home. The Colt runner from second base was heading home!

It was a nice one-hop zinger of a throw, and Earl fielded it cleanly. But it arrived a half second after the runner scrambled across the plate with the second, tying run. The score was 2–2. The runner on first advanced to third. There were no outs, and Big Foot was still up with a 2–0 count.

Coach Franklin replaced Earl with Bill Wirick. The lanky freshman pitcher still looked underweight. But new muscle was starting to show. He had gained a lot of control over his split-fingered fast ball, and his unpredictable throwing angles made him especially effective as a relief pitcher. The batters didn't have enough time to get used to him.

Big Foot gently poked his bat at the first ball Wire threw. It went to Jim Nelson in right field. As the ball took flight, Robbie removed his mask and tossed it behind him. He picked up the bat left by Big Foot and underhanded it out of the way. Then Robbie set his cleated feet firmly on either side of the third-base line, a yard in front of the plate.

But Nelson, worried about his throw home, fumbled the ball after he caught it. That left plenty of time for the runner at third to tag up and score.

Robbie moved aside as the Colt runner sprinted past him for the go-ahead run. There was only one out, and now Riverton was behind. Robbie called time and went out to console Wire.

Looking slightly confused, Wire said, "Robbie, do you know we have a no-hitter going? Three pitchers so far, a lot of walks, some bungling, *but no hits*! Three pitchers are pitching a no-hitter! And we're behind, 3–2! I don't understand this game!"

Robbie nodded in sympathy and said, "You're not supposed to mention we have a no-hitter going. It's supposed to be bad luck."

"I'm not superstitious, Robbie."

"Ah! Good!"

"Let's get this guy, then."

"Okay!" Robbie trotted back to his home behind home.

Bay High's Meat was up again. Robbie kept calling for sinking, low pitches, hoping to get a ground ball hit. Finally, on a 2–2 count, Meat smashed Wire's split-fingered fast ball directly over Wire's head. It looked like a sure single up the middle. But suddenly, there was Jonesy! He was so smooth that his sprint looked more like a glide. Jonesy gloved the ball on the fly deep behind second base for the second out. The third out came on Wire's next pitch, popped up to Mojo Johnson at first base.

Robbie was slated to lead off the Tigers' half of the seventh. *And we're behind, 3–2.* While he was quickly removing his catching gear, Mosely casually took a drink from the dugout's water fountain. He said in a low voice, "Two homers in two at-bats. And catching a no-hitter from three different pitchers! No place to go from here but downhill, Big Boy!" The last words he spat out distastefully. Then Mosely walked to the other end of the dugout and sat down.

With a sigh, Robbie picked up his bat, along with the weighted one, and walked toward the batter's box. Riverton fans were already hooting and clapping for him to hit another homer. His wrist still pulsed painfully around a bruise that seemed to darken even as he looked at it. He had gotten somewhat used to playing with bruises and aches in his limbs from all his catching this season. *But still, pain is pain,* he thought.

Before Robbie could step in the box, Big Foot called time and trotted out to Hightower. They had a short discussion. As Big Foot returned to the catcher's box, Robbie said, "Hi."

"Are you still here? We were hoping you'd left."

Robbie smiled. Then the two opponents got serious again.

Hightower wound up and threw. It was a curve ball that started out going behind Robbie, then bent and plunged toward his kneecap. Robbie scooted his legs back and nearly fell over. He just barely dodged the ball.

"Ball one!" yelled the plate umpire.

"Sheesh!" said Robbie, stepping out of the box.

"Sorry about that," said Big Foot.

"Is he going to pitch to me or what?"

"I think I wouldn't be telling secrets out of school if I told you we don't want to give you anything too good to hit."

"Why not walk me intentionally, then?"

"*I* recommended that. But Tyrone says he wants to pitch to you."

The umpire spoke up. "As soon as you two catchers are done deciding how to pitch to this batter, maybe we could get on with the game."

But at that moment, the Bay High coach called time and ran out to Hightower. He told the pitcher something brief and firm. The Colt coach walked off, calling to his catcher, "Walk him!"

"See you around, guy," said Big Foot. He stretched his arm out for the intentional walk. Hightower rather angrily threw three straight outside balls, and Robbie jogged down to first. Meat greeted him with a grunt and said, "Glad you're stopping here this time."

Catchers weren't usually expected to steal. Often during the season, Robbie had taken advantage of this by running on the first or second pitch. But he wanted to have a look at Hightower's motion first. So he was glad to see Coach Franklin giving no steal sign.

Robbie took a lead that almost forced Hightower to throw the ball over. Robbie slid back with two split seconds to spare. It was close, but now he knew how Hightower's delivery looked when he tried a pick-off. Robbie took a long lead again, but not as daring as the first one. Hightower looked over, seemed to sniff, then made the pitch to the plate. José Sanchez cracked it with a vengeance, as if it were a mosquito that had been bugging him for the last hour. But the liner went foul, two feet outside the third-base line. The Tigers were starting to get around on Tyrone the Typhoon.

Robbie felt he had Hightower's pitching motions to home plate and first base memorized now. And Coach Franklin, sharp as ever, flashed him the steal sign.

Robbie crept off first the same distance he had for the previous pitch. Hightower looked over, looked at the plate, looked over again, then started his motion to home. Robbie was off and running. He didn't look homeward but instead kept his eyes on the shortstop now coming over to cover the bag. *He's starting to reach to his right! Hook slide!*

Robbie leaned toward right field as he began his slide away from where the shortstop was catching the toss. Robbie's left toe pinpointed the smallest corner of the bag before the shortstop could swing the caught ball into it. "Safe!" the umpire yelled, flashing his arms in an X close to the ground. The Riverton fans hooted and clapped.

By the time Hightower had run the count on José to three balls and two strikes, Robbie had the catcher's on-base signs figured out. So when Big Foot flashed one, three, two, Robbie clapped and called, "Okay, José, José!" The clap and saying José's name twice meant a curve was coming.

José hit the curve right on the nose, but on two neat bounces to the third baseman. Robbie didn't run. Then he saw the ball skip off the third baseman's glove. The ball scooted into "no man's land," the area equally distant from the left fielder and third baseman. Robbie was racing around third base when the left fielder finally picked the ball up. Coach Franklin was waving and hollering him home.

Big Foot, looking ten feet tall and six feet wide in his catcher's equipment, hunkered right in front of the plate. *How am I ever going to get through that?* Robbie wondered as he got closer and closer to home plate. He was now two feet from the Colt catcher, and he began a kind of half slide, half cross-body block. Big Foot didn't budge an inch, and Robbie was stopped dead in his tracks, flat on his face. He heard the sound of the ball popping head-high into the glove of the Colt catcher.

But suddenly, Robbie saw a slice of plate between the catcher's spikes. He lunged his hand through and touched home. Big Foot whammed the tag against Robbie's upper back. The umpire was right on top of the play. With his nose just two inches from Robbie's hand on the plate, he called "Safe!"

No more Tiger runs scored that inning, but Robbie had tied the game. He put on his gear and ran to the catcher's box for the eighth inning. Robbie saw Eagle, still holding the ice pack on his wrist, talking to Cynthia. She didn't seem to be listening, however. She was watching Robbie. Robbie froze for a moment, looking at her. *Magic still around, I guess. I don't know how long it can last, but I'm sure having a day! I'm sure having a day!*

Even though the game was in the late innings, Robbie felt full of energy. The usual aches and pains seemed small now. Even the deep wrist bruise he had gotten from that wild pitch in the dirt by Markley didn't bother him. The constant handling of the ball, the drama of every pitch provided just the thing he craved. He suddenly realized he was exactly where he wanted to be. *Catching is the perfect position for me*, he thought. *The perfect position.*

Chapter Nineteen

Neither team scored in the eighth inning, though each left men on base. Wire got out of the ninth inning on a pop-up and a double play. It was now the bottom of the ninth, and the Tigers started to zero in on a tiring Hightower. John Roberts tapped a blooper to short left field, but Bay High's shortstop made a fantastic skidding catch. Jim Nelson got a nice piece of the ball and sliced a single to right. Wire tried a half-swing bunt, but the Colts' alert third baseman caught the soft liner in the air and nearly doubled Nelson off first. Jonesy then kept fouling Hightower pitches off, ten in all, until he drew a walk.

Mojo Johnson had been studying Hightower closely all afternoon. He had struck out the first two times up, but put good wood on the ball in his last at-bat. He took two close calls. His old catcher's eye was still working—both pitches were balls. Now he just wanted to meet the ball, to make honest contact. It had to be a strike-zone pitch.

Hightower's fast ball came right down the pike, and Mojo slapped it right back at the mound. The ball hit the rubber and bounced high in the air. The shortstop caught it, but too late to stop the runners. The bases were loaded, and Robbie was up.

Eddie Trent, sitting in a front row seat by the Tigers' dugout, gazed fondly at the baseball drama before him. Robbie Belmont was batting for his fourth time. It was the last of the ninth inning with two outs, the bases loaded, and the winning run on third. There were a few college and pro scouts in the same section as Eddie. He'd been hearing their excited comments throughout the game. They had come to evaluate Hightower, and their reports were, in fact, very favorable about him. But Belmont was a surprise to them. They were counting their blessings for being there—and counting the number of years Robbie had before graduating. "If he's this good now, what'll he be like in four years?" was the most common comment.

Eddie recognized that Robbie was having one of those magic days. Many times during this game, Eddie had recalled the few magic days in his own baseball life. There was the day in the seventh grade when he'd hit three home runs and a triple on an ordinary Wednesday after-school game. He remembered how calm and playful he had felt during that game. It was as if pulverizing the ball was the most natural thing in the world to him. That was a day when everything seemed bathed in a blazing white light.

Hightower threw Robbie a blistering fast ball, high and inside, for the first pitch. But Robbie let it pass.

The New York Titans' scout, Mack Doogan, was sitting a row behind Eddie. Doogan leaned forward and said, "At least they can't walk the kid intentionally this time!" Eddie nodded agreeably to Mack.

Hightower tried another fast ball on Robbie for the second pitch. But he was so leery of Robbie's bat that the ball went too low and outside. Robbie now had two balls and no strikes on him.

Robbie's magic day was touching off memories in many people throughout the stadium. They recalled their own great days competing. A little girl thought about the one time she finally beat a bully named Sissy in a race during gym class. Ralph Butler was thinking about his first high-hurdles race. He had defeated the top-ranked runners easily, even though they were two years older than he. Brian Webster was recalling that one glorious day of whiffle ball, the only time he had ever beaten Robbie in his life. And Robbie's mother found herself reliving a swim meet during her sophomore year at college. Her physical development finally seemed to catch up to her never-say-die heart. She was racing the backstroke when suddenly her arms loosened up and gave her more stretch. She won the race—and clinched the overall victory for her college swim team.

The magic was still thrumming through Robbie as he waited for Hightower's next pitch. The temptation to shoot for another homer was hard to resist. But Robbie knew all he needed for a Tiger win was a clean hit—*any* hit.

Hightower was taking more time than Robbie liked, so Robbie stepped out of the box. Big Foot went out to the mound to go over the signals with his pitcher. Then he jogged back to home plate.

Hightower reared back and threw a fast ball past Robbie that showed why so many scouts had attended this game. Despite his weary arm, Hightower had just thrown the fastest pitch seen in the entire game. *Hightower's a competitor— that's for sure!* thought Robbie. The count was now two balls and one strike.

Robbie guessed Hightower would have to come into the strike zone with the next pitch. A 3–1 count with the bases loaded would put too much pressure on the pitch after that one.

Everyone in the stadium was standing now. Their cheers and shouts were deafening. As Hightower reared back once again, a thought snaked through Robbie's mind: *The magic is gone. The magic has left me!*

The ball zoomed in again, a carbon copy of the previous throw. Robbie swung late. He just barely ticked it, fouling it into the stands behind first base. *Late swing. Feeble swing. No magic in that swing!*

Robbie was feeling very tight. Hightower, on the other hand, seemed to puff with confidence. He had just checked the game's biggest hitter with two big fast balls.

Robbie cast a quick look at Cynthia. She was the only one in the stands, it seemed, who was not moving. She just looked at him. His eyes swung to the right a bit where he noticed Eddie Trent standing, smiling, and clapping. *Maybe the magic is gone. But I still have to give one hundred percent!*

Robbie stepped back in the batter's box. The count was 2–2. Now it was Robbie who was in the hole, one pitch away from a strikeout. He had to protect the plate. Hightower, looking more imposing than ever, began his wind-up. *He's just blown two fast balls by me*, thought Robbie. *So this will probably be more heat!*

Robbie started to step forward early, looking for the third straight fast ball. Hightower's arm whipped ferociously over his head, but the ball was floating in as slow as a firefly. *Change-up!*

Robbie was caught off balance. His body was too far ahead of the ball to get full power behind his swing. His leg had stepped forward, but his hands still had not committed. His ever-sharp eyes had adjusted to the unexpected slow ball, tracking it for dear life. It was a change-up curve, twisting slowly toward the low outside part of the plate. *It might be called a ball. But it's too close. I have to swing!*

Robbie's legs and body were out of whack, it

seemed. His arms also were too far ahead of the pitch. Only his wrists were still holding back, and now he put them to work. Just as the ball was crossing the heart of the plate, Robbie concentrated all his strength into power-wristing the ball. Every part of his body but his wrists felt foolish. So now he let his wrists crank the bat.

The slowness of the ball was such that Robbie could actually *see* his bat hitting it. He tagged it solidly, punching it into right field. The crowd gasped as the Colt right fielder ran in to catch the ball before it touched the ground. Robbie's foot had just touched the first-base bag when the ball finally sunk. It bounced on the sweet earth before the right fielder could catch it. *Magic enough for me!* Robbie thought, jumping for joy.

A huge ovation erupted. The Riverton Tigers could almost feel it tingling on their skin. They leapt on each other and screamed. Then they rushed Robbie, cheering and reveling in his game-winning hit.

The mob scene was cut short when the Tigers realized they hadn't shaken hands with Bay High's team yet. The Colts were milling around the diamond, wondering if they should forget the after-game ritual. Mad Dog had sunk to his knees on the left-field foul line. His head was hanging low. When the Tigers began shaking hands with the Colts, he slowly got up and joined the crowd.

The handshake Big Foot gave Robbie was firm. "Boy, you had some game, guy!"

"Thanks. You guys played us tough. It could have gone the other way just as easily. Anyway, it was a pleasure playing against you. Great catching."

"Same to you. Three pitchers and a no-hitter! Seems you were the common thread there."

Hightower gave Robbie a polite handshake, looking distantly over Robbie's shoulder. But then he turned his face and gave Robbie a close-up look. With a sudden jolt, Robbie saw the agony the guy felt. Hightower's look was tired and strained, but respectful. "I didn't know what to throw you. Next time we meet, I'll have to have a new pitch!"

"Try a split-fingered fast ball. With the kind of pitches you already have, it'd make you even tougher than you already are."

"Maybe I will. Great game." And Hightower walked away.

Coach Franklin came over and ushered Robbie into the dugout. From there, they headed through a tunnel into the locker room. The coach spoke to Robbie as they walked. "There's going to be an awful lot of scouts who will want to talk with you about your future plans, Robbie. I recommend you not say anything to them just yet. You go on and relax and enjoy yourself in the locker room. Let me handle them for you now. I'll pass on anything important to you. Beautiful game, son. Especially that last hit. It was all wrist, wasn't it?"

Robbie was amazed. *The coach could see that?*

Smiling, Coach Franklin put his arm around Robbie, then stared into space for a while. After a moment, Coach Franklin pulled some candy corn from his jacket pocket. "My county championship victory corn," he said, popping it into his mouth. "Haven't had any in many years! Mm-mm! It's good! Have some."

Robbie took some. Nothing ever tasted sweeter.

Chapter Twenty

In the locker room, Robbie was in a daze. *Everybody's being so nice to me! Did I just do what they said I did? I sure did. Man!*

It was a happy atmosphere, but not a wild celebration. A number of the Tiger players felt bad about not batting well. But they had gotten a few hits the last two innings, and the fielding all day had been first rate. And winning the county championship certainly felt good. They could show how well they hit next weekend in the state regional tournament.

Eddie Trent came into the locker room and congratulated everyone. When he got to Robbie, he pointed at a bruise on Robbie's wrist. "Seventh inning, right?"

"Right," said Robbie.

"I got two bruises right next to each other against the L.A. Lions yesterday." Eddie rolled up his sleeve and showed Robbie two purple-black splotches on his right forearm. "First inning," he said, pointing at one. "Third inning," he said, pointing to the other.

"Those are beauts."

"Anyway, congratulations, Robbie! Especially on your catcher's no-hitter."

"Catcher's no-hitter?"

"Different pitchers, same catcher, no hits. And with three pitchers, not just two!"

"Thanks, Mr. Trent."

"Hey, it's Eddie, remember? We catchers—"

"—have to stick together," Robbie finished for him. The two catchers laughed.

"See you again, Robbie," said Eddie, heading for the exit.

"Looking forward to it, Eddie," Robbie called after him.

Before leaving the locker room, Eddie once more shook Gus Franklin's hand. Then he was gone. Robbie knew he had a game later on.

Once outside, Robbie got a big hug and kiss from his mother. Then she looked him in the eye and said, "Two home runs, a game-winning single, and a steal. Oh, Robbie, your father and I are so proud of you!"

Funny, thought Robbie. *Eddie Trent talks only about my defense and pitching calls while Mom talks only about my offense. Strange how two people can see the same game differently.*

St. Simon Belmont gave his son a firm handshake. "Your mother's right, son! What a day! It was just beautiful!"

Robbie saw Josh, Brian, Melinda, and Ralph crossing the parking lot. "Mind if I catch up with the gang?"

"You go ahead, Robbie," Ellen Belmont said, beaming. "Enjoy yourself!"

Robbie picked up his duffel bag and hurried off to meet his friends.

"Hey, hey, hey!" shouted Brian. "If it isn't the MVP of the county championship game!"

"Aw, go on, Brian," said Robbie. "It was a team effort and you know it."

Melinda interrupted now. "You're right, Robbie. It *was* a team effort. Besides, we all know who *really* was the game's most valuable player." Melinda paused to make sure all eyes were on her. "Me and my stat sheets!" Then Melinda burst out laughing, and the others joined in.

"You got a point there, Melinda," said Robbie, only half-kidding. "You got a point."

They all headed toward Brian Webster's station wagon. Robbie got in front, and Josh, Melinda, and Ralph climbed in back.

"Let's go, Bri," said Ralph from the back seat. "And see if you can get some *real* music on that radio of yours."

Brian turned over the engine and pulled out of the parking lot. Then he pushed one of the FM presets. The deejay was introducing a song.

"And now, a blast from the past! Here are the Salty Dogs doing their big sixties' hit, 'Love at a Distance.'"

Brian was about to push another button when Robbie reached over and stopped him. "Hey, leave that on."

"Crank it!" shouted Ralph from the back seat.

"There's a great guitar solo in the middle of this tune." Brian turned up the volume.

The station wagon pulled up to a stoplight. A second later, Eagle Wilson's car moved alongside. Cynthia Wu was sitting in the seat next to Eagle. His bandaged wrist was resting on top of the steering wheel. He rolled down the window.

"Cynthia says to meet us at Swanee's."

"Swanee's it is!" shouted back Robbie.

The light changed, and Robbie watched as Eagle's car slipped ahead into traffic. Cynthia turned around in her seat and waved back through the window. The image of her waving stayed with Robbie. "Love at a distance is better than no love at all," wailed the singer on the radio. *Can't argue with that,* thought Robbie, easing back into his seat.

The purr of the motor and the warmth of the late afternoon sunlight made Robbie sleepy. Some of the excitement had passed now, and Robbie was beginning to feel tired from the game. His eyelids got heavier and heavier. Then they closed.

Suddenly, Robbie was standing in the batter's box at Birchmere Stadium. This was the home field of the New York Titans. Over 75,000 fans were there. Behind the plate was Eddie Trent, catching for the Titans.

"Good to see you again, Robbie," said Eddie through his iron mask.

"Thanks, Eddie. Good to see you, too."

"Welcome to the big leagues, kid!"

Behind the Iron Mask

Great baseball action and off-field drama await you in all six of Gary Carter's Iron Mask books. Future Hall of Famer Gary Carter, a ten-time National League selection as catcher for the annual All-Star Game and the 1984 All-Star Game MVP, has closely consulted on this baseball series. And he has written a personal introduction for each book. Follow the exciting exploits of Iron Mask series' hero Robbie Belmont as he rises from high-school star...to college record breaker...to promising pro!